Wren

RR Carroll

DEDICATION

This story was written in tribute to the memory of the kindest person I have ever known, and the love of my life.

Sherry Francis
1946-2012

She was my most honest critic and my greatest fan. No man can ask for more than that from the one he loves.

May God keep her close.

ACKNOWLEDGMENTS

In recognizing the contribution to this work made by my editor, Sandra Sargus, all I need to say besides thank you is that it would not have been completed without her indefatigable help and encouragement.

Her support is of the kind that helps us all to realize how connected we are, and how much we need one another in this life.

୫ଠ

A special thanks also to a great design artist, Nichole Wicks for a most appropriate cover for this story.

PROLOGUE

A wingless angel

The messenger

M Y NAME IS ÁGIOS CHRISTÓFOROS. Not really, but that's the name I will use for the purpose of telling this story. I have to admit that Greek names have always appealed to me, and that particular one is especially compelling. An understanding you will reach much further on.

I'm what you might like to call an angel; that's right, from up there. I don't have a real name; the fact is that angels don't need names. The One Who Calls us doesn't need reminders. We're just spirits in His service. Envision if you will a school of fish in a vast ocean, millions swimming together constantly in an elegant swirling dance, coordinated choreography, each and every one an exact

1

copy of the next but yet everyone different as daylight from dark. I know that doesn't make any sense, but sometime in your future it will; trust me on that. But all that sameness changes when we have something God wants us to do. The grand swirl becomes a single spirit. That spirit then takes a name, and a form. Call it required baggage when we travel to places in God's Infinity.

As I write these words, I'm moving around in your terrestrial house. I have been for a while. He sent me to escort a released spirit on a mission. I'm his guardian angel; yes there are such things. Usually these assignments are routine; I would say boring, but I really don't think I should. If you've done one you've done hundreds, but this one is different. The fact is I cannot remember any other quite like it. And that's why I'm telling the story; it's a tale with a lesson. You might say a moral truth that's worth a notice, worth remembering. Maybe the term message is a more apt descriptive. You see the One that assigns angels to these errands, I can assure you, enjoys sending messages, and so that's what this narrative is intended to do.

I must warn you; however, up front that storytelling is not my natural calling. I'm afraid this is a detail you may recognize soon enough. But, understand nonetheless, that like I said, this is a story worth the telling no matter how well I tell it.

Let me note also that my name will not always be Ágios. My physical form, as well as the name by which I am called, will change with the circumstances and with the time and place that me and my charge find ourselves. Oh, and Luke, that's his name, will not always be called Luke either. Confused? Okay, good.

It is my intention to stay out of the way as much as possible in this tale, and hope that you can figure out the message on your own. Just know that angels, by their very nature, are a privileged bunch. We get to see things that mortals, restrained as you are in your physical shells, will walk right by without notice. It is part of the job so to speak; part of our divine toolkit. So, I might decide to drop a few crumbs on the trail to help keep you from getting lost along the way.

With that said though I promise that I will not be a busybody. If I sense you struggling don't expect me to jump in and hold your hand; this is not the yellow-brick road. There are some things you will be expected to work out on your own. I'm going to, as much as possible, blend in; to fulfill the terrestrial human that everyone thinks that I am. But be assured that whether you recognize me or not, I am there in the scene, always doing what He wants me to do; always attempting to deliver His message.

Before I begin though, while I know I shouldn't do it (I did say I would stay out of the way), I'm going to give you a hint at the start.

There's something that all angels know that humans do not; or at least, most of you do not. That is that when man commits a wrong against his fellows; when man breaks one of God's rules, especially the one about love thy neighbor; God responds to the transgression by tossing a seed of redemption out of Heaven towards earth. In other words, there is always a chance that the wrong done can be righted; that the one gone astray has a chance, by the choices he makes from then on, to correct his previous blunders. If the seed is nurtured, that is if it takes root and is given a chance to grow; then the original offense against God can be rectified, and the wrongdoer will atone and can be redeemed. That's the word for this story…redemption.

These Divinely distributed seeds are on the air, all around

you at every moment. Every wrong can be righted; every single one. This wonderful choice is always available to you, and only has to be recognized for what it is and the chance seized in order to bring forward God's saving grace. You see, what I am attempting to get across is that there is surely a second chance. Take it from an insider, God is always ready to let man begin again; just for the good of it. We angels have always wondered among ourselves why it is that most humans never figure that out. But, that's another story for another time. For now, let me begin with this one: let me deliver the message…

†

PART ONE

SPIRIT EATERS

Walking backwards

"If you cannot bring justice directly to those who have wronged you, then bring a fearful vengeance to those nearest them. Punish their people harshly so the villains will know and feel deeply that their actions have consequences for their own kind; the wrongs they bring to others will sooner or later be visited on their houses; there will always be justice, even if it appears riding upon a horse called revenge."

Winter Campaign log, Indian Territory, 1868
Brevet General George Armstrong Custer,
United States Army, Seventh Calvary

Camp Supply, Ind. Ter. Nov. 22, 1868 (Sunday)

Too Cold for Gary Owens

Battle of the Red Moon

THE SHRILL BUGLER'S NOTES OF OFFICER'S CALL echoed off the jagged limestone cliffs just above Camp Supply. The musical message, muted by the heavy flakes of falling snow, made their way to the officers and men of the Seventh Cavalry scattered about on the white powder below. Lieutenant Luke Erin anticipated what the meeting would produce as he hurriedly shouted orders to his sergeant and fumbled with the tarnished buttons of his collar. The handsome young officer tried to kick the white powder from his boots as he moved toward the general's tent. He could see his major ahead of him already entering through the flaps, and so he quickened his pace.

He was confident that they would receive the orders to form their columns and begin the long-anticipated mission; a mission which had as its military objective to scorch the earth and kill any and all Indians that they could encounter. As he ducked his head and moved to take his place around the general's table, Lieutenant Erin sensed an atmosphere of festivity among the officers of the Seventh Cavalry. They quietly, but good-naturedly, jostled each other like school boys preparing for a wrestling match against their rivals. Major Myers nodded at Luke with a signal of soldierly recognition and a slight but perceptible smile. It was a sentiment that had been long absent between the major and his subordinates in the months leading up to this morning.

The jocularity among the men ceased abruptly as the general made his entrance, and, without any recognition of his assembled officers, tossed several dog-eared maps on the table. Captain Benteen dutifully began to arrange the jumble for the briefing.

"Gentlemen," Custer began in a soft, undramatic voice without looking up, his stare fixed on the maps before him spread out on the rough-hewn table.

"Gentlemen, we are about to do what we came to do. We are about to take the hell that the red man has brought to us and our kind on the plains, and deliver it back to the very ground on which he places his lodge in these same snows that fall in such divine glory and portent outside this tent. To his sacred home in which dwells his life's blood we will make his kind feel the chill of the winter that he has never known before. Before we are through, his wives will scream and his children will cry, just as he has made our children do with such bloodthirsty abandon."

General Custer paused as he looked up slowly. For a long and intimidating moment he surveyed, one-by-one, every officer that surrounded the oblong briefing table. His gaze was determined, and there was no mistake that the flamboyant commander was gathering in all his resources for the battle that was soon to follow.

"There is to be no quarter," he finally continued, "no

hesitation. In a word, there will be no mercy shown to those who have shown no mercy to the scattered and isolated frontier families across this land."

Custer snatched up one of the maps in front of him before he resumed. "If you and the men you command do that which is expected of you as soldiers of the United States, the future of these lands for the white man will be assured as will the future of the red savage that stand in the way of that destiny."

Silence followed as General Custer sat down slowly, and haphazardly pitched his broad-brim hat near his feet on the soft soil floor under the table. Several officers by reflex flanked the commander on both sides and peered over his shoulder at the map that the general had used for emphasis.

Custer leaned back in his camp chair and suddenly broke into a broad smile like a man who simply could not contain his merriment. He forcefully brought his finger onto a crude, hand drawn version of the terrain around Camp Supply. Slowly and methodically he began to trace a route that extended along, what all the officers now assumed, was to be the path of the march until it reached the flowing waters of the Washita River. It was a river that coursed, twisted and turned, looped and double-looped up like a snake under a boot.

"South by southeast is our line of march," the general declared. "Make all your preparations commencing immediately. Have your companies in formation and ready to march before first light."

"General, if I may comment..."

Custer made no recognition of the officer's request, cutting him off as he continued with his instructions.

"All necessary supplies to sustain our column for at least four weeks in the field will be required, gentlemen," Custer paused, looking with an intense stare at the officer who had dared to interrupt.

"And major," he said, "if your comment has anything to do with the heavy snowfall, you may keep that to yourself. The days of hesitation and frustration ended yesterday. The entire point of General Sheridan's directive for the winter campaign is now being fulfilled by God's grace, and we shall take full and forceful use of that grace to our advantage. The Indian will soon feel the wrath of the white man's God by the means of the sword of the Seventh Cavalry."

The general crisply saluted his officers. "Gentlemen, these meetings are now terminated. I suggest you get directly to your duties."

✝

Nits make lice

Red fires on white snow

Log: Lt. Luke Erin, Company E, Seventh Cavalry, U.S. Army
Camp Supply, Ind. Ter. Nov. 22, 1868 (Sunday evening)

It is cold; it has snowed for two days and it is still snowing. The flakes are as lazy in their descent as some of our troopers in their duties. Cleared a bit at noon and began to warm, but still it snows lightly. Gave orders to Sergeant Major O'Grady to have all the horses dispersed to find what foliage they can. Had a noon officers' call meeting in General Custer's tent. Received our orders to prepare to march tomorrow at first light. Some of the enlisted are grumbling about moving in the weather, but most are anxious to get at the Indians (if we can find those rascals). Meeting with Captain Myers followed the general officers' meeting. My Capt. is as enthusiastic as the general about the fight to come. He says the red devil has had his way far too long. Meyers is a hard type. Asked him about what was to be done about the women and children when we attacked the Indians' camp. He didn't answer my question directly, but said only "that nits make lice." I took that as a "damn them all." I want to make note here should someone read my account at a later time that this attitude about non-combatants, especially from a superior officer, troubles me somewhat. There are many in the troop, mostly enlisted men, a most primitive group by in large, who would kill a squaw to make pouches from her breasts; but I expect a higher notion from the officers. For me, I know what I know. I can't kill a woman or a child, Indian or no Indian. If the time comes when this is expected of me, I can't say now what I will do; how I will avoid the decision. Some of the troop finds their inquiries answered by what they believe to be their Creator. I no longer find any comfort in that source.

ಬ

LOW AND MUFFLED GRUNTS OF PROFANITY were passed up and down the length of the column like vermin under a camp blanket. The dark of the new day obscured the sources of muted insubordination so the officers ignored the grumbles and growled their orders without paying heed to potential rebellion.

Everything about preparing the troop to leave Camp Supply and begin the march south by southeast was made painful by the twofold difficulties of the biting cold of the dark pre-dawn and the ugly, but deep beauty of the white powder that threatened to extend beyond the tops of the troopers' black leather riding boots. The mules stiffened like stone statues as the company's skinners tried to force the shaggy, brutish creatures into harness. The normal routine of cussing and working took on much more of the former as General Custer grew more impatient with each passing minute of delay.

More than once, before the column was prepared to depart, Custer rode off in the dark as if to leave all behind and take on the mission single-handedly. Each time the officers cringed as they heard, as if from a ghost, cruelly shouted commands to mount the horses and take to the march. Each time there was no immediate response. The general, mounted on a big grey steed he called Dandy that was as nervous as its rider, reappeared and all made show of working with animated, but superficial haste. Even the mules seemed to sense the impending wrath from on high and finally begrudgingly submitted their rigid shoulders and frosty muzzles to the inanimate cold of the leathers and buckles.

Lieutenant Erin found his sergeant major and with simply a look of pleading ignited the wrath of the diminutive but mighty headman of the enlisted troopers.

"Any man or animal," he roared, "not ready in five minutes will be left for camp duty," his bass tone resonating though the crisp pre-morning air over the length of the frozen assemblage. The response to this ultimatum came as a half-hearted "ready sir!" that seemed to change very little about the pace of preparation. Once again the general impatiently made his horse pay the price as he put the sharp rowels of his spurs to the sides of the already edgy mount. The horse and its rider made their way off into the distance, as if to leave for the battle with or without his command in train.

༄

Log: Lt. Luke Erin, Company E, Seventh Cavalry, U.S. Army
Camp Supply, Ind. Ter. Nov. 23, 1868 (Monday)

The march began abruptly and with difficulty on all sides so I write my entry hurriedly. No time for a cooked breakfast, only a hard biscuit made harder by the cold. Snow, deep snow everywhere, cold to the bone plagued all officers and men alike. But all must be ready by first light so with only the low grumblings to lessen the chill, all the men set about loading the wagons, three per company, and hitching the teams. Somehow the tasks were finally accomplished and the columns, four abreast, were prepared to commence at six o'clock. Trouble was we couldn't see our trail or any landmarks because of the heavy snow. General Custer, astride his magnificent grey steed, took the lead and with compass in hand we were off to take the Indian to account. I am a bit frozen like all my comrades, but I am well, and ready to advance on our enemy.

❧

AT LAST, GENERAL PHILIP H. SHERIDAN'S GRAND WINTER CAMPAIGN; against the hostiles was to begin. His subordinate, Brevet General George Armstrong Custer, would take the point of four columns, and thirty wagons and ambulances and lead them stubbornly through the deep resisting white powder that seemed to, paradoxically, both restrain and oblige their purpose. The general was shrouded in his finest and heaviest buckskins, shielded better than most against the bitter air of the early day. What a magnificent and proud man the general appeared to Lieutenant Erin as he rode ahead of all the columns. The young officer believed that his fellows of the Seventh, led by such a commander as this, were to be written into the pages of a magnificent history: a history that would surely unfold in the next few days of this bleak November, 1868.

As the two officers rode there was only silence between them. It was a contagious silence that stretched all along the line of 900 officers and enlisted men, civilian guides and interpreters, Indian scouts, rough-and-tumble teamsters, and one essential blacksmith. Luke kept his eye on the general well in the lead, his features mostly hidden from scrutiny by his ponderous wraps. The commander periodically raised himself in the saddle, surveying with his compass and then pointed the way forward. The great mass of somber military moved on his authority, like a circus line of plodding pachyderms.

Occasionally the silence, accentuated only by the softly falling flakes, was rudely punctuated by the crack of the teamsters' whip, giving emphasis by the likewise stinging snap of the crudest language. Luke was pleased that these ragged and violent men where always far in the rear. His upbringing in the house of his gentle and religious father forced his distaste of their constant and meaningless rough chatter that only served, for the lieutenant, to fill his thoughts with a base opinion of mankind. Their curses seemed to have no good purpose other than filling the world with ugliness.

Erin glanced at Major Meyers; an indirect glance without speaking. He had something to say and the thought wouldn't give him peace. The major's flippant remark about the killing of non-combatants at Camp Supply wouldn't stand for a proper officer. Luke could not easily dismiss the thought of the moral wrongness of taking the lives of the innocents in this conflict over the land and a way life. How could an officer, he wondered, infused with the sense of honor that was attached to his core of beliefs just as the insignias of rank were attached to his shoulders, be brought to such a thing? The question haunted the lieutenant as the two rode to their duty.

As the column plodded on through the winter bleakness, Luke struggled to make the initial words of his inquiry pass his lips. They wouldn't come. Then before his mind could restrain his words, Luke heard himself say "Major."

"What is it, Lieutenant?" the major's response was as cold as the air that enveloped the riders.

Luke turned toward the major who stared straight ahead. "Kind of cold, isn't it sir?"

The major ignored the comment, and Erin let the moment pass; resigning himself to wait for another time. The heavy wet snow persisted and the young officer, sitting stiffly and erect in the saddle, suddenly felt the cold soaking his soul. He twisted and looked over his shoulder at the mass of armed men slogging across the trackless Indian Territories; moving obstinately toward some point on the Washita River where they all would be expected to do what all soldiers are expected to do.

ॐ

Log: Lt. Luke Erin, Company E, Seventh Cavalry, U.S. Army
Ind. Ter. Nov. 24, 1868 (Tuesday)

Marched 25 miles today. We are somewhere north of the Canadian River, I.T. Reveille at three o'clock. We started on our scout. It snowed all day with a deliberate purpose and intensity. None of us in the column could tell the road ahead. It was only because of the forward scout and the compass of the general that we had any faith in our heading. All the beleaguered troops, as did I, dreaded the cold and wet night before us that would certainly follow the day's long march. Our bed for the night was over a foot of new snow. Miserable does not portray the discomfort of lying on the cold ground in wet clothes although the abundance of wood all around us did afford some comfort and light, not to mention the blessed warmth. No news of Indians this day. The talk of the officers this evening suggests that they have all gone south. All fear that they have once again eluded our pursuit and will frustrate our desire to engage them in battle. There is, for the moment, not a high degree of confidence that we will soon discover them. But, we will soon resume the march. I am well.

℮ℭ

THE NUMEROUS FIRES BURNED INTENSELY, SEPARATING THE BLACKNESS OF THE CAMP into sections of human gratitude for the light and the warmth that the flaming logs provided. Like all the men who had suffered the day's march, Luke sat rigid before the glow of his own light and comfort and stared at the three other officers gathered near him, their faces appearing and disappearing with the errant light. Second Lieutenant Edward Law and Captain Robert West, both of Company K, had joined Luke and Major Meyers. The weather had thankfully moderated during the day, and the intense discomfort of the initial blizzard had abated; a welcomed thaw in body and mind had begun to have its salutary effect. There was an atmosphere of weary cheer among the officers as they sipped on the black, hot liquid in their cups. Captain West had produced a bottle of spirits to enhance the flavor and effect of the bitter coffee and smooth out the edges left by the day's trek.

The Kid Law, as everyone called the miniature, baby-faced second lieutenant, was the first to break the silence of the gathering.

"Any sign of the red devil today?" he blurted without preliminaries. At first his abrupt expression brought no response; but finally, with more cheer in his voice than normal, the captain answered cryptically.

"You'll have to ask Elliot, Kid."

"I would," he answered, "if I could find him. I haven't seen the major all day. Where do you think he is off to?"

"Now where do you think, Kid?" Major Meyers, with a bitter sarcastic tone, joined in the discussion. "The general sent him off on a scout. I expect he'll send word when and if he makes contact."

"I sure hope he does just that, and soon would be soon enough for me. I'm restless to deliver a bit of soldierly justice to these heathen." The enthusiasm in the kid's voice was at the moment comical and welcomed by the senior officers around the intense glow of the cottonwood logs. His kind, fresh for the fight because he doesn't understand the fight to come, is easy to lead, the senior officers knew, is easy to command.

"Well let's hope this damnable snow melts before we have to charge into some God-forsaken Indian village," West interjected; redirecting the topic back to the one constant and known condition of all those who huddled around their bright comfort.

Luke stood up and shed his heavy coat. The fire and the suddenly rising temperatures were bringing quickly a welcomed change to his body. With a long, thin stick he poked at the blaze, sending sparks rising hurriedly into the night air. Suddenly he heard a shout from the neighboring fire. There seemed to be a considerable stir and the raising of voices alerted that something was about.

"Suppose, by the sound of the excitement, we're to get some news shortly lads," Meyers offered without moving his comfortable position of crossed legs and a full coffee cup with a taste added.

The young second lieutenant reflexively jumped to his feet, and as he clumsily bumped into Luke in the dark, said he was going to find out what was going on. As the kid disappeared through the smoke, Luke commented, "My notion is that we've got a scout back from the hunt, you suppose, Captain?"

"Looks like that's the case, Lieutenant. We'll know soon enough I suspect. If I were betting man, I'd bet we will hear the officer's call on the bugle in a few minutes."

શ

Log: Lt. Luke Erin, Company E, Seventh Cavalry, U.S. Army
Ind. Ter. Nov. 25, 1868 (Wednesday)

Marched 18 miles today. Made camp on the north side of Wolf Creek. A hard day on men and beast alike. The game here is plentiful. We killed buffalo, rabbits, and deer. The bounty was appreciated by all the men. The other good was that the snow finally let up and it is steadily getting warmer. All hope an easier passage on the morrow. Brisk news from Major Elliot's scout arrived in camp late this day. A large number of Indian pony tracks discovered heading south by southeast. This is our own direction. All spirits were immediately lifted as the report was given to all the officers by the general himself. There will be a 3 o'clock reveille again so we may proceed with all speed to intercept the Indians. With their bellies full, the enlisted are particularly excited at the prospect. The day of reckoning rapidly is approaching. I am well and definitely warmer this night.

એ

"REVENGE, WE'LL HAVE IT SOON ENOUGH NOW," shouted Major Meyers as he and Lieutenant Erin mounted for the day's march.

The excitement had been renewed among the officers and enlisted of the Seventh Cavalry; as well it had to all that had marched in the hard weather since leaving Camp Supply. The mood of drudgery through the bitter winter was replaced with a nervous anticipation of the chase and the hunt that was finally on in earnest. Major Elliot, taking with him three troops, a few white scouts and two Osage Indian trackers had headed off earlier. The general had made Elliot the lead and all expected a good report on the hostiles' whereabouts to come back to the main body by mid-day.

Some officers were saying that what was about to take place was justice served at long last for the Indian depredations in the Kansas territories up and down the Big Smokey River. But the major, Luke knew, put it more correctly with the word revenge. He knew that justice wasn't what was surely to follow. Revenge was a much sweeter condiment for the banquet that the general had in mind when they reached the villages of the Cheyenne, which no doubt now that they would very shortly do.

રૂ

TWO WAGONS WERE BEING SUCKED DOWN BY THE QUICKSAND, and there was little the cussing muleskinners could do about it. Captain Winslow ordered them abandoned and screamed the orders to transfer as much of the ammunition as possible before it disappeared in the mud. The captain looked to the southeast and tried to get the scent of blood that he knew must be on the air.

He was looking in the direction that General Custer and his elite companies had taken not an hour before. The news from Major Elliot's scout had brought a most unusual use of profanity from General Custer as he shouted out the order for all to mount.

"I smell their blood boys, I smell their blood!" he almost screamed as his horse spun around and made circles in the snow. "Now, quickly let's get to this bloody business."

Lieutenant Erin was riding just to the right flank of Major Meyers as both men simultaneously caught the first sight of Major Elliot and his troopers just over a ridge. The general was pushing his mount hard to join Elliot, and soon all the officers were collected in a mounted circle surrounding Elliot.

"Report, Major," Custer said as he swung dramatically off his horse and motioned for all to follow.

"Over a hundred Indian ponies, General; at least that many, maybe more crossed that stream just below us not more than half a day ago. They're off in that direction," the major pointed first to the small tributary and then swung his arm around from the Antelope Hills to what all knew would be the direction that would take them to the snaking Washita River in the distance. Every scout and Osage Indian tracker had advised the general that this is where they would find the Cheyenne and their allies encamped for the winter. And that was precisely where Major Elliot was now pointing.

General Custer remounted and gave a theatrical salute to all around. "We will have them!" he shouted as reflexively his officers mirrored their commander. All re-formed their columns and Lieutenant Erin could see Major Elliot and the scouts move off in the lead.

"Blood scent is on the wind, Lieutenant," Major Meyers said to Erin as they led their squadron and spurred their horses to a quick pace. They were soon crossing the narrow icy stream, and there in the mud of the mushy snow the white riders added the tracks of the horses of the Seventh Cavalry to those of their red enemy. Orders came from General Custer that the column would stop for only two hours so that all the troops could take a bit of coffee and prepare for the arduous night march that would follow.

Each trooper spent his few minutes of respite fortifying his spirit and checking and re-checking his Spencer carbine and the heavy Colt revolver at his side. The one hundred rounds of ammunition he toted was a weight he tolerated. These were the tools of the trade and each man wanted to make sure that they would be put to proper use come the new day.

The general ordered that the main wagon train would fall behind with only a small escort, and the fighting squadrons would move out at a quick pace. Major Elliot's lead squadrons, with their Osage and civilian scouts, had already departed as the light of the day faded and dusk began to control the skies.

"We'll hit the heathen from every point on the compass," General Custer spoke softly but with sternness. All of his officers gathered around their commander as he drew a crude circle that represented the Cheyenne gathering of lodges, not far away.

ॐ

Log: Lt. Luke Erin, Company E, 7th Cavalry, U.S. Army
Ind. Ter. Nov. 26, 1868 (Thursday)

I am writing this entry shortly after the battle on the Washita. Oh what a grand victory General Custer has proclaimed! Major Elliot had found them, had found the Indians' lodges, in the late of the night, and had sent us word by his scout Corbin. Little Beaver, our trusted and magnificent Osage tracker set all to a high state of readiness and excitement when he quietly returned to General Custer's lead troopers and reported that the hostile camp was close to hand. The general had asked him how he knew, and holding up his hand for silence Custer heard the soft tinkling of a bell. All recognized that a Cheyenne pony herd was near. Then, as a point of confirmation, we heard a dog give alarm just over the ridge and the unmistakable cry of an Indian infant drifted up from the valley of the Washita. The general motioned all to back away from our forward position so we could receive our orders and plan of attack. I need not say that all the men of the Seventh were as tense as a wound spring and were anxious to do their duty.

✝

White flag on Red Snow

Hide in the tall grass

"MY AUNT VIOLENTLY SHOOK THE SLEEP FROM MY BODY. As I stared at her, she asked me if I felt it? if I could feel the thunder in the ground? the rumble coming from mother earth? I didn't know what she meant, but she told me to leave the lodge and do it quickly; to run fast like the antelope on the prairie to the high-ground and there to hide in the tall grass. She shook me again, making sure I understood. I will never forget the words she spoke. "The soldiers are coming, hurry yourself, the soldiers are coming.'"

Recollections of Running Turtle, Cheyenne girl
Black Kettle's band, Washita River camp
November 27, 1868

✝

"RUN LITTLE GIRL. RUN!" shouted Blue Bird Flies, as she pushed her gentle and beautiful young niece through the opening in the lodge. Running Turtle, with the weight of a heavy blanket of drowsiness, struggled against her terror, but was true to her name as she instinctively headed towards the cold waters of the Washita River. The frozen ground was hard and each step brought a loud crunch as her bare feet met the slick, rude surface. The ragged ice was slicing small cuts between her bare toes, but Running Turtle was not aware of the pain or of the slight trickles of blood that came with each bit of damage to the soft flesh. Like a deer with an arrow in its side, the Indian girl, barely a woman, was leaving a slight trail of red on the virginal ice and wet snow as she fled the horror that was coming over the rumbling earth.

Her heart, almost overwhelmed with panic and confusion, expanded into her throat as she became aware of the harsh reports of the rifles from the direction of the tall cottonwood trees; woodlands that had always provided comfort and safety, but now portended of the dreadful fantastic about to come. She altered the direction of her flight, and as she ran she recognized, also in frantic escape, two of her cousins headed towards the ridges just south of the lodges, up and along a long and gentle slope into a scraggly group of scrub oaks. It was Little Wolf and Jumping Man, she was sure of it. The two stumbled as they ran. Running Turtle saw Little Wolf fall, and momentarily consumed by the snow, disappear from sight.

As she watched the two young men flee the chaos,

Running Turtle visualized them as they sat near to her in the lodge of her grandfather, Black Kettle, the night before. The chief's lodge, with a great fire warming all that gathered, had been happy with laughing and celebration at the return of Black Kettle's son, Blood Feather. She could see her father's proud face as he told all of the great triumphs his Dog Soldiers had won during the cycle of the last moon. They had brought ponies taken from the Utes, and two young ones taken from the white invaders above the Canadian River. Running Turtle, could now recall as she ran, the look on Black Kettle's face; a look she didn't recognize at the time of celebration, but now in her own panic was clear. It was a look of sadness, sadness so deep that it looked out through a fog of fear; she was sure of it now.

"Come with us!" she heard Jumping Man shout as she struggled in the grass over-burdened with white powder on the slope. "This way, run this way!" he shouted.

But the cries of her cousin were cut short by the report of the rifle from just behind the girl, and she watched with a blood horror as the image of the living boy/man from the night before suddenly became wide-eyed with shock; a shock that ends all shock. Jumping Man tumbled backward and disappeared into the ground cover without another sound. Running Turtle, moving with the instinct of a herd animal, abruptly changed her direction of flight in a desperate attempt to avoid the same fate. She wildly hurried along the ridge, hoping she was running from the source of the danger she could feel now was so close. For a reason only known by the spirits, she suddenly recalled the words that her aunt had screamed as she pushed her from her sleep and into the cruel cold.

"Hide in the tall grass! Running Turtle; hide yourself in the tall grass!"

With that notion her legs involuntarily collapsed from under her body; and like a fawn in the presence of wolves, the young Indian woman lay still on the cold snow, her innocent ears listening to the chaos that rumbled like distant thunder from the village below. Her fear again competed with memory, memory of the last several days among her father's lodge.

She could see her grandfather, the man who always rode stiff and straight astride his favorite horse, as he crossed the turbulent waters of the Washita. A man of great and enduring pride was returning with all the other chiefs. The men had been to pow-wow with the blue coats; eagerly making the effort to convince these dangerous men that the Cheyenne people wanted to live in peace with what the Indians called their white brothers. Black Kettle was old, but his steadiness and gentleness made his people feel safe from whatever threat would come from the whites and their army.

Lying still in the grass and snow, Running Turtle could yet hear his quiet voice as he told all the impatient ears about the threats the white soldiers made against the Cheyenne and their friends. Threats of revenge, or as Black Kettle said, what the white man called justice. Because of the war actions of the Dog Soldiers and Blood Feather, the white soldiers would come for revenge.

The young Indian woman, her body numb from the cold of the ground that now replaced the warmth of her blood, began to cry softly. There was sadness about all her senses. Her skin was cold, her ears hurt from the violent noise that penetrated her soul, her eyes could only see the barren white ground and the dead yellow of the winter grass; and the acrid smell of gunpowder filled her nostrils like the stench of a decaying animal and stained her tongue with a bitter taste.

Then Running Turtle felt the thing she feared, coming near. At first she wasn't sure what it was, but she felt it. Her body stiffened in silent expectation. Suddenly she knew that it was the spirit of her forefathers who were coming to claim her; to take her to the place of sweetness and the great happiness. The ground was trembling; she could feel it vibrate as if it was trying to consume her flesh and bones; to cover her over with the shroud that took away the air and the light.

The shout, more like a hoarse scream, from somewhere above the girl abruptly dispersed the gathering spirit that had only a moment before seemed so present, so real, so kind. The now alien sound of words, harsh like a cold wind on bare skin, brought the horror back and placed it next to her. She rolled over slightly, just enough to see the nervous prancing of the horse's hooves close to her place of hiding. She dared not look up. Running Turtle knew she had been found; she gritted her teeth and waited for the sting of the sword point or the blast of the gun that she would never hear.

But then, rather than the wound of quick death, she felt the hands grab her hair from behind and jerk her up from the snow and onto her knees. The shouts from the man were both gruff and demanding but with a peculiar tone of gentleness; more a strong command than threat. As she felt the arm encircle her waist, Running Turtle looked down and could see the deep blue of his jacket sleeve with some strange markings in gold on the cuffs. From behind, the voice kept instructing but the sounds were of no use to her; they brought only noise to her ears, an echoing noise without meaning. She let herself go limp; the notion to struggle against the force was cancelled by the wish for all of it to end. She felt the power pull her closer, and she could feel the warmth of his body on her back and the sudden rush of cold air on the back of her legs. There was a long moment that seemed to have no end. She was caught in a trap, but all was still, suspended. Finally she was pushed strongly forward, her hands reacted instinctively to catch her fall and her forearms where buried in the fresh snow, her hands grasping clumps of the grass to fix her to the ground.

The pain came then, but she didn't cry out. She closed her eyes and listened to the sounds of the rifles that now, with mercy, had moved farther away, moving down the Washita River with the flow of the red water. There were no longer any screams from the direction where Running Turtle had fled the soldiers. Suddenly she saw it, and then she felt it. It was like a puff of white smoke that floated in the air. It settled all around where she lay.

And then she was aware that the force in blue that held her no longer did so. The Indian girl didn't want to move though. She was so very tired.

The nervous prancing of the horse's hooves again filled her ears and then, like a story told by her aunt, she felt as if she was flying, flying on the wind down the slope toward her village; what remained for the moment of the village of Black Kettle, her grandfather, the village of Running Turtle's people.

&

"WELL, WELL, WELL, WHAT DO WE HAVE HERE LIEUTENANT?" Sergeant Major O'Grady stretched his ape-like arms upward towards Lieutenant Luke Erin to take his bundle.

"Looks like a prairie plum to me; that it does." The sergeant lowered the girl to the ground gently, but didn't loosen his grip on her arm.

"She was up on the ridges, Sergeant, hiding in the tall grass," The lieutenant reined in his horse as the nervous animal spun around in place.

"Take her and put her with the other women and children. Tell the corporal of the guard to take care with her, she's quiet but I think maybe a bit dangerous. Where is Major Meyers, Sergeant Major?"

"He's with the other officers sir; all officers are ordered to rendezvous with the general down at the oxbow of the river. All lodges and supplies are to be burnt to cinders. The general will leave nothing behind but ashes."

"What about the hundreds of Indian ponies, Sergeant? Are we taking those with us?"

"No sir. Only a few of the best for the officers, and a few so the captives can ride with us. The rest are to be shot. Those animals will never carry the raiders again; no sir, they won't."

The sergeant major's scream was muffled, but intense; and he instinctively turned loose of Running Turtle's arm as she bit deep into his hand. In an instant she was running back toward the ridges. Sergeant major shrugged and gave a slight sigh as he looked up at Erin.

The officer couldn't help himself, and he grinned slightly and shook his head. "She should have been a warrior," he said as he spurred his mount to renew the chase.

The lieutenant's horse quickly overtook the girl, and she was retrieved in an agile swoop of the officer's arm. Running Turtle offered no resistance as the young girl settled across Luke Erin's leg. The young woman appeared strangely comfortable and pushed her body into a secure union with the young cavalry officer.

"I'll take her myself to the corporal, Sergeant Major," he shouted as he approached O'Grady, "I think you've had enough of this one."

Luke rode by his sergeant and nodded. The sergeant major offered a brief salute in return and moved towards the gathered Indian ponies while rubbing the sore spot on his hand. He motioned for the twenty enlisted men with carbines to follow, and the assassins began to circle the nervous pony herd of the defeated Cheyenne.

✝

Black Tongue Woman

Burn the damn thing!

RUNNING TURTLE moved into the sanctuary of the arms of her aunt, as the Indian women and children were gathered by the soldiers like a flock of chickens. For the moment, the two women were content to merely be together. It was a small comfort given the chaos of the last few hours of fright. Running Turtle looked all around for any signs of her family. Where is her grandfather? Where is her father? Her cousins? There were no men of her tribe, only blue coats that were consumed by the task of deliberately destroying the life of her people. Everywhere there was fire and bitter smoke. The desperate looks on the faces of the Indian women portrayed the scene that played itself out before these helpless mothers; a scene that could never be imagined in any future, but only lived in a present horror.

Black Tongue Woman moved closer to Running Turtle

and gently nudged her aunt aside as she embraced the young woman around the shoulders and pulled the trembling girl close to her body. She chanted in an almost imperceptible groan and began to sway slightly from front to back. As she did, the hoary medicine woman reached deliberately forward and caught the lower edges of Running Turtle's buckskin dress. She gripped the irregular leather between her forefinger and thumb and pulled it up over the woman's leg with a slow exposure of the flesh underneath. As the covering moved upward it began to reveal the dried red of congealed blood on the inside of the young girl's thigh. The old one's chants increased in volume and began to resonate with a vibrating intensity that signaled to all the Indian women a message that was lost on the surrounding soldiers, and only the Indian women understood.

As a soldier began to move closer to the huddled women, Black Tongue Woman ran her finger through the red stain on Running Turtle's leg and then lowered her dress to cover her leg. Running Turtle didn't look at the medicine woman. If she had, she would have seen Black Tongue Woman put her finger into her mouth and close her eyes. The chants continued until suddenly the old woman screamed with a force that caused all the soldiers to raise their rifles as if anticipating an imminent attack of Cheyenne warriors from some unknown direction. The other women joined in the chanting and, too, began to sway in the same motion as Black Tongue Woman. The only one that didn't move or utter a sound was Running Turtle. She knew what Black Tongue Woman had determined, and she shivered in the cold because of the fate that would be hers.

"What do you suppose that's all about, Sergeant Major?" Lieutenant Erin said as he dismounted and, with reins in his left hand, motioned with his right toward the gathering of captives.

The sergeant major just shook his head. "Far be it from me, Lieutenant, to know the minds of these savages. Suspect they are calling out the devil to deal with their enemy. That's what our women in Ireland would do. There'd be banshees about as soon as the sun did set; I can tell you that, sir."

The lieutenant turned to remount his horse, but then paused, and began to approach slowly the tightly huddled women. The sergeant major dutifully moved along with his superior. The fires consuming the lodges were roaring; and the crackling of the flames sent sparks, smoke and an eerie noise up to the heavens as a background to the continuing mournful chants of the closely gathered Indian women. The orchestrated and intermittent explosion of soldiers' rifles signaled the beginning slaughter of the Indian treasure nearby. Above the den, all about could hear the ponies moan as their mates fell around them. Lieutenant Erin drew close to the tight circle of women and came within a few feet of the young Indian woman he had shortly before brought in as a captive.

Black Tongue Woman stood up as the lieutenant came near and deliberately moved toward the young, tall officer of the 7th Calvary. One of the guarding soldiers reacted to the movement and started toward the old woman and held up his rifle as a warning, but the ancient one paid little heed to the threat and continued to move closer to the lieutenant. Lieutenant Erin motioned for the guard to stand down; and, as he did, he found himself face-to-face with the deeply folded and brown, weathered skin of the Cheyenne medicine woman.

The old one raised her eyes to meet the look of the officer and began to speak. She looked intently at the soldier that towered over her in a way that left no doubt that she was telling him something. She spoke the same words over and over; the message took on the rhythm of chanting. Their mutual gaze locked as if the universe had destined these two to speak without understanding; to touch without feeling.

Erin called out to his sergeant. "Sergeant Major, get scout Corbin. I want to understand this old woman. She's trying to tell me something."

"He's just over there, Lieutenant; he's part of the killing detail of the Cheyenne ponies. I'll send the private to get him. But sir, you're needed by the general."

"I know, Sergeant. I'll go shortly enough. I just want to know what this old one is saying. Get the scout, Sergeant."

Black Tongue Woman had her eyes closed now and her words, her chant, had reached an intensity that captured Erin's attention above all the commotion surrounding them. He watched the old woman for a moment longer, but turned away as he saw Nathaniel Corbin approach. Before he could take a step he felt the light touch of the medicine woman's hand on his sleeve. There was no restraining force about her touch, but the lieutenant felt as if he had been stopped by a power. He turned completely back to face the old woman who now was again looking into his eyes. Erin felt that she was looking at his being, his history, or what his father would have said was his soul.

"What is it you need, Lieutenant?" Nat Corbin said as he clutched his carbine in his left hand and slipped a long bladed bloody knife into his belt. "This old crow givin' you some grief is she?"

"No, it's not that. I think she wants to tell me...us something. Look at her. Is she in a trance? You see? Look at her eyes. They're as black as the bottom of a well at noon."

Nat Corbin stepped up next to Lieutenant Erin. "Lieutenant, all these crones are like that. They sit around all day and look at the spirits. All these Indians see some spirit or another, but this one sees more than that. Her kind sees the past and the future; or so they say. I betcha she sees your future. That's what she's saying. Let me hear for a minute; maybe she'll let me know."

Black Tongue Woman turned without looking away, and immediately Running Turtle, absent any sign of command, rose as if she floated up from the ground and moved the few paces to be next to the woman who never ceased to chant her message. The young woman kept her head tilted slightly downward, but as she came in contact with her kindred, she raised her eyes without moving her head and looked first at the scout, and then the black of her gaze fell on the young lieutenant.

"I think the young one's smitten, Lieutenant; yeah, she is taken by you, sir. That she is."

Nat Corbin held up his hand for those in the close circle to listen. As he did the medicine woman again touched the sleeve of Erin's coat. Just then another volley from the nearby slaughter broke the silence as if to underscore the message that Black Tongue Woman was sending.

"Scout, you getting any of this? What is she saying?"

"Not much. I don't have much trouble understanding the Chiefs, but this one, this old spirit is calling out in dark and ancient tongues." Scout Corbin rudely grabbed the old woman by the arm and said something in Cheyenne that Erin didn't understand, but the reaction was immediate. Black Tongue Woman quit speaking and turned her dark eyes on the scout as if laying a malevolent curse on her enemy.

She began speaking again in an entirely different way. "There, Lieutenant; now she's making some sense. Hold on!"

Corbin said something to the old woman and she

responded. The scout spoke again, and, again Black Tongue Woman answered. Then both were silent and just stared at each other as if what they had shared was not permitted to be repeated.

"Well scout, what is it?" the lieutenant said looking from one to the other.

Finally, Nat Corbin took a step back from the medicine woman and indicated that Lieutenant Erin should step back as well.

"Lieutenant, I'm not sure you want to hear this. And, I'm not sure I want to try and repeat what I think this Indian witch said." Scout Corbin paused as if he expected to be released from this unpleasant assignment.

Erin looked first at the now silent scout and then glanced over his shoulder at Black Tongue Woman who had returned to the side of Running Turtle. There the old one embraced the young Indian woman as if shielding her from an expected harm.

"What did she say, scout?"

Again the scout appeared to not want to respond. At last, he spoke. "Lieutenant, I may have not really understood what this old creature said; but, if I did, I think she said that you have eaten the young Indian girl's spirit. I think that is what she said, I do."

"What?" Erin suddenly appeared to Corbin and the sergeant major to be particularly agitated. "Did you say, ate her spirit? That's what you said, right?"

"Yes sir, that's what the old medicine woman said. I think. And there's something else she said. She said that the young woman has eaten your spirit too." The scout took a step back and turned as if he was going to walk away from the discussion and this unpleasant duty and get back to killing horses.

"Scout Corbin! Wait a minute. Explain this spirit eating thing to me. And make it quick, I've got to rendezvous with the other officers and the general."

"Lieutenant, I'm not sure myself. But what I think it means is you two are now one."

"What? That's supposed to make sense, scout?"

"I know, Lieutenant. These Indians are in a different world, sir. These strange notions are not for us to understand; they're, well, to put it right and simple, they're crazy by our measure of things."

The sergeant major moved to the right shoulder of Erin and interrupted. "Lieutenant, not to push it, but the general is waiting; don't think that's a good idea, sir."

"Yes, Sergeant, I agree. Okay, scout, that'll do. One other thing though, and put it into just a few words. How are we one? I mean how are we joined?"

"Sir, do I have your permission to speak candidly?"

"Of course you do. What is it?"

"Sir, that Indian girl, according to that medicine woman; well sir, she's going to have a child."

"So, what's that got to do with me?" Erin made a move toward his horse.

Nat Corbin made a point of spitting out a wad of soggy tobacco before he spoke. "Sir, the child will be yours."

Lieutenant Erin mounted his horse without another word and put his spurs to the spirited animal and rode in the direction of the Washita River; towards the group of officers gathered around their triumphant commander at their center.

Nat Corbin, standing close by Sergeant Major O'Grady watched the young, proud officer ride away as the two shared a brief glance. It was a look of seasoned recognition between the two warriors.

"Sergeant Major," an excited corporal abruptly pushed himself between the two men, "look what I found outside the lodge of that old chief, you know the one they call Black Kettle; the one they shot in the river." The corporal held up a smoothly carved length of the branch of a cottonwood tree. The pole was about five feet long and on one end was tied a rectangular piece of white cloth.

"This here flag was lying in the snow, Sergeant. You could hardly see it lying there in the white snow. Damn thing looks like a peace flag, Sergeant. I would like to hang on to it; you know kind of a souvenir thing, you know?"

The sergeant major grabbed the flag and its primitive pole and held it up to the sun, the light of which was barely visible through the thick grey smoke of the fires that blazed fiercely all around the men. Abruptly he shoved the flag and its crude pole back into the arms of the corporal.

"Burn the damn thing, Corporal; burn the damn thing. The general gave orders. No souvenirs. Burn the damn thing! And get back to killing those damn Indian ponies. Get back to the killing you damn fool so we can get out of here."

The corporal looked stunned, but did as the sergeant ordered. As he walked back to the slaughter, he tossed the symbol of peace onto the fire, and moved on.

✝

Gone to Texas

HARD RIDE TO GRACE

Texas road

GONE TO TEXAS. These were the words that John Cotton Straw had crudely scrawled with lime chalk, on the barn door of his hardscrabble fifty-acre sweet potato farm in the southwest corner of Rhea County, Tennessee. On a prematurely cold September morning Daddy John busily loaded his life's product, blood and hardware, onto a sturdy Studebaker wagon and put the long whip to a matched and prized yoked oxen team, directing the slow and lumbering but steady beasts onto a trail that would lead to the Texas Road. To hear Daddy John tell it, his family was finally headed to the Promised Land.

Ever since the end of the great conflagration, the Tennessean with the blood of his Irish ancestors coursing through his veins had read from a small, leather bound book emblazoned with the gilded title the *Emigrant's Guide to Texas*. Daddy John kept the book in a cotton sack securely tied with a red silk ribbon and always close to hand. He would preach from that volume to any and all in the family who would heed or listen as if the words he read were the very words of Scripture. By tallow light most every evening the patriarch of the Straws would memorize sections of that little book and, as such, he could fluently recite chapter and verse, which given any provocation, he often did. On those occasions when there was scarcity of human ear to heed his clarion call, he delivered his secular sermons to his livestock who, he was convinced, appreciated the wisdom and thus were as anxious as he to move beyond the barrier of the Mighty Mississippi and the constraints of the southern way of life.

His own life had become this dream and his dream was given authenticity by the incantation of the words the *Lone Star State*, a land that was yet far away from where the likes of the Straw clan were or of what they knew. But it was this unknown that pulled at him like a mule pulls at a plow; steady and slow, but relentless. For Daddy John it was not a matter of if, only a matter of when he and Mama Straw and their young-uns would put the whip to oxen, and point the dull beasts down the Texas Road.

✝

CHRISTÓFOROS' BURDEN

A tale told in silence

THE MASSIVE, awkward wagon pulled by the lumbering pair of oxen the family called Cherry and Peach, was no more than seventh in the line that waited for the ferryman's benevolence and the slow fording of the Red River at Colbert's Crossing. The morning was clear and crisp, and the prospect for travel on the day was good. The journey had been hard down the Texas Road through the Indian Territories, but that harshness was little more than a cheerless memory for the migrant family now that the sweet sight of Texas was before them on the other side of only a muddy river.

The weeks of somber travel had taken a toll on the family from Tennessee. The dreaded pox had claimed little William Tyler somewhere east of Fort Smith even before the family had made it to the well-worn trail south to Texas running slightly east of Fort Griffith. The boy and the fear of contagion he carried were quietly concealed from all eyes but God in a dirt mound with a crude wood cross and a quick prayer alongside the wagon ruts that marked the trail.

Old Sam, their worthless hound had, too, treed his last squirrel and chased his last possum as he shared Willie's fate as if the old hound wanted to provide company for the tragic lad in the afterlife.

Life and supplies on the long trail from Tennessee ran low and what remained of the sugar that sweetened Daddy John's coffee ceased to be, long before the flies were done with the carcass of the family's favorite dog or the maggots had finished their repast on the Daddy John's youngest son.

John C, the first-born man-child of the clan, also had developed the croup as the wagon inched its way closer to the sweet promise of Texas; and Mama Straw, without comment, dutifully administered what remained of her self-concocted syrupy remedy to the convulsing boy. The braking handle on the wagon added to the misery as it had busted two days before, sliding down the rocky grade just north of the big river; but Daddy John said it could wait until the wheels of the wagon tracked through the longed for sweet Texas clay.

The potato farmer from Rhea County was anxious; it was obvious to his wife that the patriarch could smell the land he had so longed to see. It rose gently on the south bank of the Red River as the swift current willfully pushed the sand from bank to bank. The Straw's wagon moved up and now was the sixth in line.

Mama Straw, leaning to one side, could just make out the little box with the tow-headed boy that sat next to the ferryman's station just ahead. From her high perch she was sure the creature was naked, and she wondered what the commotion that surrounded the ferryman and the box could be about. She could see that the boy was the focus of conversation as each wagon, in its turn, lumbered by the point of departure.

Then finally the Straws claimed their place at the head of the line, and Daddy John reached deep into his coat for his money pouch to pay the toll. He fingered gently the few gold coins he possessed hoping that the fee would not be too dear. The hard dollars would be sorely needed in this new land. He fixed his gaze on the ferryman's broad frame waiting for the news of the price of passage.

"Mister. Where are you headed?" the man said softly, almost as an apology, his eyes staring and fixed a good foot below where Daddy John sat on the board of the wagon.

Daddy John didn't speak quickly, which was his nature, and glanced at Mama Straw as if he wanted her to interpret the question if not tell him what he should say in response to the ferryman's inquiry.

He returned his own gaze to the burly man that stood four feet below his line of sight and spoke, "To Texas," he said with a shaped tone of authority in his voice.

"Might I inquire as to where in Texas, sir?"

Daddy John again threw a quick glance at this woman. "A place called Young County; we are headed to the Evans Track. We've got a claim to a league or more when we get there. Why do you ask, mister?"

"You're settlers then?"

"Yes sir, we expect to be soon enough."

"Christian folks too, I assume to be the case?"

"Why yes sir, we certainly are, Calvinist by our take on the Bible. May I again ask the purpose of this survey and your name?"

"My name is Benjamin Franklin Colbert," the ferryman said formally, "and it's about this boy you see before you; the naked boy in the box next to your wagon. He is a half-breed heathen; I'm guessing about five or six years in age and mostly Cheyenne mixed in with a tad of white blood I'd guess. I know this because I'm of the same mixture exceptin' my injun blood is Chickasaw. You see a group of murderous, no-account Panateka Comanche left him just across the river." The ferryman stepped back from the wagon and pointed towards a bend in the flowing water just upstream.

"It was about three days ago; them savages were makin' their way west I reckon, been raidin' poor settlers I'd bet you. Why they didn't kill the poor lad I have no notion. They usually do that if they can't make the young-uns' people pay a ransom. Must have seen a sign or somethin' in the boy that warned them off, can't figure though. The Comanche been raidin' in these parts since the moon grew full. They hate the Cheyenne as much as the Cheyenne hate them. No matter about that now; this boy needs a home."

The boy John C went into a coughing spasm and Mama Straw pulled her oldest closer to her chest and rocked him gently all the while looking intently first at Mr. Colbert and then at the naked, pale red boy in the crate. Daddy John turned his gaze on his wife and slowly shook his head.

Then he said, "Sir, I don't understand all this. We just want to pay our ferry fee and cross into Texas. We ain't lookin' to take on any strays."

The ferryman pretended that he didn't hear Daddy John's protest and stuck the toe of his boot into the side of the crate and forcefully spun it around so that the broad face of the bare-skinned boy revolved towards the Straw's wagon. The youngster looked up slightly in reaction to being disturbed, and Mama Straw could see the green eyes clearly; noting as she did the calm reflected in them that seemed to stare without seeing. The boy didn't blink but gazed intently at the big woman's round and sunburned face as it loomed above; his scrutiny touched somewhere deep in the big woman. It made her look closer at the young boy in the crate; and, as she did, she noticed an odd dark indigo tattoo of what resembled some kind of bird laid out across one side of the boy's shaved head.

"And sir, there's more to this story that I will say is beyond strange, even for me and this wild place, 'cause I can tell you folks that I've seen much mystery on this river. What I mean is I've been watching that boy since them heathens dropped him over yonder. I hate to tell you, but some that's come through here said they'd bet the boy would be taken by wolves or coyotes or somethin' eat him if someone didn't take him out of that sad box. I started over there more than once myself; but, I don't know what, but somethin' always made me turn back. As strange as it might be, I took on a feelin' of fear. You know, the kind that warns you in your gut against somethin' fearful."

Daddy John abruptly cleared his throat trying to free his family from this unwanted delay, but the ferryman ignored the evident plea.

"Then, mister," he continued, "may the blessed Mother Mary curse me if what I tell you now is not the God's truth, the God's own truth, I swear to you. You see, it was right along about sunset yesterday that I looked over the waters at the boy's crate when I saw this man standing near to the lad. From where I am now that man appeared to be a giant. Even from way over here you could tell, he must have been over seven feet tall if he was an inch. He was dressed in buckskins, you know the kind them buffalo hunters on the prairie are inclined to wear. His hair hung down near to his waist in loose strings that flowed with the air as it moved. He was a sight, I promise you." Mr. Colbert took a step back again and spit tobacco juice in the dust before he continued his tale.

"Well sir, that giant reached down and picked that boy up, crate and all, and hoisted him onto his back with both hands holdin' the box. I looked on with unbelieving eyes as the giant stepped into the flowing water of the river and started for this very ferry crossing with that naked boy and that box the lad lived in perched on his back like a sack of grain. Now here's the thing about it mister." Colbert hesitated as if he was trying to find the words that would make this story believable. His muddy eyes shifted toward Mama Straw with a pleading for understanding that was clear in his gaze, and then he turned back to the driver of the wagon.

"You have to understand that the river is deep through here. I don't know exactly how deep but it floats the barge, that's for sure. I've never seen a man walk across it, no sir, never. But praise all that's holy in this life, that giant of a prairie man did just that. I'm here to tell, he brought that boy clean across that river, through that swift and dangerous current, over all that must be quicksand; and it took him near on an hour to do it too. By the time he reached over here, the wagons were backed up for nearly a quarter of a mile. Nobody, and I mean nobody, moved while that man came across that water with that boy on his back. They all just watched in silence the spectacle that was that crossing. When that prairie man in buckskins finally came out of the water, you could see clearly the man had done all that was in him. I swear I thought he would fall over and die right there, but without a word he sat the boy and crate down right where you see it now." Colbert paused and spit again.

"What was the man's name?" Mama Straw asked, breaking the spell and looking down on the teller. "Where was he from; did he say?"

Mr. Colbert paused for a brief moment before he answered. He looked at the boy in the crate. "Ma'am, don't know. The giant just stood there dripping wet for a time, staring at the lad, before he turned and started walkin' away. I called out to him, but he never turned back. He just faded away, come to think on it, he was there, and then he wasn't; that was it."

Daddy John, with his hands still holding the reins, looked at Mama Straw. Hesitantly he said, "What did the boy do, Mr. Colbert?"

"That's the other part, mister. I've never seen a young lad as calm through the whole time as that boy. He never said a word. The fact is he hasn't said a word in all the time he's been here. To tell the truth, I don't think the boy can talk, injun or otherwise. Not a word or a grunt, nothin'. He just sits in that damn box, excuse me mum, quiet as a dove in the morning mist. Some of the families through here have been pitchin' food into his box and he takes it, but that's it. He just sits there in his own filth. I'm at my rope's end, mister. I've got to get shed of him soon," he said as he paused to collect his thoughts.

When Mr. Colbert spoke again he revealed a bit of anger in his words, "or I'm going to pitch the crate, boy and all, in the river and be done with it. Mister, I tell you what, your ferry fee is on me if you will take the boy on," he paused and spit again, "and for that matter I'll give you ten dollars, hard dollars too, for your kindness."

"Sir, we can't..." Daddy John practically shouted his response to the ferryman's proposal.

"Daddy John," Mama Straw forcefully interrupted her husband, "you hand down this shawl to cover that cherub with."

"Mama..."

"Mister, hand down this shawl!" Mama Straw took the garment and folded it precisely and handed it to Daddy John who passed it on unenthusiastically to Mr. Colbert.

"All right, Mama, but we ain't taken that lad on. Ain't we got enough of a burden already?" Quietly he looked at his wife and in a soft voice he pleaded, "Why, it ain't been two weeks since we put one of our own in the territorial sod east of the Fort?"

Mama slowly shifted her big body to the side so she could let her son rest on his own. Without a word, the matriarch of the clan positioned her heft so she could descend from the wagon bench to the ground. Daddy John appeared to be nervous at the prospect but, as usual, he didn't interfere with his woman's intentions when he could see they were resolute.

Once the big woman reached the ground Mama Straw quickly arrayed the fine woven cloth gently over the boy's shoulders. She wrapped the soothing fabric about the naked frame the way a mid-wife would wrap muslin around a newborn. The boy emitted what sounded like a faint whimper but he didn't resist or show any other sign; there was no fear in him it appeared.

Mama Straw then put her strength to work and lifted the boy clear of the filth and the wood crate that had been his home. She forcefully kicked the crate several feet off the road and took the boy's limp body to her bosom just as she had John C's moments before and fixed her gaze up at Daddy John who appeared to be frozen in place, mesmerized if not terrorized by the scene that played out below where he sat, still holding the reins and waiting to go to Texas.

"Daddy John, this boy is blessed by the sweetness of our Savior Jesus Christ." Mama Straw gently rubbed the boy's markings on his head. "He's going to Young County with the Straws."

"Mama, we can't take..."

"Mister."

Daddy John, with a tinge of anger said, "Mama, you're just missin' young William. That's all. Now put that tyke back in the box and let's be crossin' the river. We'll leave the ferryman some money for his care."

"Mister, you've heard me. This child has our Lord's blessing, and now he will have the Straw's."

As the big wagon pulled clumsily up the south side mud road of the Red River, the boy, Mama Straw already called her *little saint*, rested without agitation on the lap of the large but gentle woman. She stroked the boy's head, massaging the strange dark sign on his skull. She knew there was a message there; she just couldn't imagine what it would be.

Daddy John was as silent as a bois d'arc post in a snowstorm as he whipped the oxen team on a west-by-southwest tack. The river slowly faded from view and the wilderness slowly came into focus. The Straws had come to Texas; it had been a hard ride to grace.

✝

A GIANT'S RETURN

Birds that don't sing

AS THE WAGON plodded along a trail that was only faintly visible, Mama Straw was the first to catch sight of the figure in the distance. She nudged her husband with her elbow; and, as he grunted a response, she nodded her head towards the man that appeared like a giant as he stood out before the primal red glow of the sun. The great ball was ending the day by slothfully burying into the dust of the frontier directly in the path of the wagon.

"Do you see him, Daddy? That man way up yonder, do you see him?"

"Yeah, I see 'em. Slide my shotgun closer to me, Mama."

Mama Straw did as Daddy John asked, and they both kept their eyes locked on the tall figure up ahead. The man didn't move, but he didn't seem to pay any attention to the approaching wagon either. It took the lumbering oxen almost fifteen minutes to draw the wagon within hailing distance of the man who, during the whole time, stood as a statue, as if he was cut from the sandstone under his feet. The rock of a man was just off the trail as the wagon pulled so close to him that Daddy John reined in the oxen and slowed to almost a stop. As he did, the giant finally looked up, and met the gaze of the travelers. At first he just stared at the couple on the seat of the big wagon as if he was expecting them or that he knew them as family. Finally the stranger spoke in a soft, but oddly deep and resonant tone.

"How's the lad doing?" was all he said.

For a very long moment Daddy John and Mama Straw only gawked at the strange man, neither one comprehended at first what the foreigner was asking. Mama Straw noticed that he was not only very large in stature, but was of a particular handsomeness even though all about him was rough, like a man of the wilds and a product of the dangerous land they were now in.

All remained silent only staring at one another. The stranger didn't repeat his question, but stood erect and still as if he would wait through all eternity for a response to his inquiry. His broad smooth-skinned face appeared to present a slightly benevolent smile.

"And what lad would you be referring to, mister?" finally Daddy John answered with a tone that was meant to sound with authority but only served to reveal the nervousness of the Tennessean.

Mama Straw slid a bit closer to her man, and not waiting for an answer from the stranger said; "You mean the little Indian boy don't you, sir? The orphan we picked up at the river, that's the one you mean, isn't it? You're the one the ferryman told us about, aren't you? The big man that crossed the river with the boy on his shoulders, that's you, isn't it, sir?"

The stranger appeared a bit pleased at the recognition by broadening his smile that now was almost a grin.

"You have nothing to fear from me, and yes, that's the boy. Is he well and safe?"

At the question, the giant turned his gaze full on Mama Straw, and she saw into the stranger's eyes. They were eyes like she had never seen before. They were of such an intense blue that they seemed to give off a glow of light that sparkled as if there was something in them beyond the man himself. The big woman involuntarily took in a sharp breath that almost choked her. When she first tried to speak the words caught in her throat, but finally, clearing her throat, she muttered; "The child is safe, sir; the child is well and safe. He is one of us now. He is safe."

"That I can see, woman. And yes, I am the one who brought the boy to you, and I am happy that he is one of you now. May I inquire what you call this little one?"

Daddy John looked inquisitively at his wife. They had not thought of a name for the unspeaking child; they only had cradled him as they traveled to their new home on the frontier.

Mama Straw, without returning her husband's look; responded to the tall one.

"I think we shall call him Little Jack. Yes sir, I think that is his name; Little Jack. We are Tennessee folks and Andrew Jackson meant much to our kind. We will call this boy Jack in his honor," she said as she turned to face her man. "Right Daddy?"

Daddy John only nodded.

The stranger reached into a pocket in his leather shirt and retrieved a small object. He took a step closer to the wagon box and reached out his hand toward the driver. Daddy

John instinctively pulled away, and Mama Straw could feel her man stiffen against her big body.

"It belongs to the boy you will call Little Jack. You must keep it until he is ready to receive it. He will tell you when that time has come. Take it now, I ask you to do this."

Again the man extended his arm and turned his hand up to the sky and opened his fingers to reveal a small carved figurine in the palm of his hand. Daddy John, with some hesitation, reached out and took the object. When he did he saw that it was a piece of green stone that had been fashioned into the crude shape of an owl. As he fingered the polished nugget he noticed how warm it was. It was almost hot to the touch of his fingers. Daddy John turned it over in his grip and finally handed the little stone bird to Mama Straw. She fingered it as her husband had; turning it over and over as if she vaguely recognized the shape.

"What is it, mister?" she said finally.

The man ignored the question, but continued. "And, take care, there will be another who will seek after the child. Be on your guard of those who offer themselves for his instruction, for he will not speak until the day is chosen. I shall be near until that day arrives; but I will not be a nuisance to your life, only watchful of the boy."

With that the giant man turned to walk away. As he took the first step Mama Straw called out in a forceful, but nervous voice. "Wait, mister, wait. You know this child. You need to tell us who he is, and who you are. I believe we have a right to know these things."

The stranger turned slightly and again looked at Mama Straw with eyes that spoke on their own.

"I think you know, I think you know the nature of the child. That is enough for now."

"Mister, we are in need of an extra hand to help us

establish our claim on these lands; would you have an interest in the job?" Daddy John almost shouted the words as he looked cautiously at Mama Straw who nodded slightly at her husband who took it to be her approval.

The question seemed to catch the stranger off guard and he paused for a long moment before he said; "My name is Ágios, and I am new to this land; but I will help you if you wish. Settle on your claim and I will return when the time is fitting.

With those words the man who suddenly was no longer a stranger turned; and, with long gated strides, slowly moved off at a right angle to the trail. As Daddy John and Mama Straw watched the man called Ágios disappear from sight, the sun finally finished its descent and dropped below the prairie, only leaving a faint glow that signaled an end to the day's travels.

There was nothing to do now but to prepare for the night ahead, so Daddy John nudged the wagon into a grove of cottonwoods on the side of a slight but adequate stream running softly over a limestone bed of rocks.

When the team had been hobbled and put to graze nearby, and the fire built for cooking, the Straw children began their nightly games about the wagon. Mama Straw sat Little Jack next to the fire. Once she thought she heard him emit a slight whine, but she wasn't sure whether it was the child or some wild creature in the darkness. He made no expression, but seemed to be as contented as any child she had ever seen. The big loving woman kneeled beside the lad and stroked his hair away from the strange, mysterious mark on his skull. As she did, her other hand went into the pocket of her apron; and she rolled the small stone owl about in the fabric, unseen by the boy. Mama Straw felt the lad slightly move his head against her hand as she continued to gently brush his hair with her fingers. But, there was no other sign from this small half-blood creature. Without thinking, she stood up and looked out into the night in the direction where the stranger had moved away. At that moment a slight wind with a strange unexpected chill to it passed over her, and she reacted with a slight shudder. The big woman from Tennessee went back to her chores in the promised land of her husband; but her thoughts would not leave the giant man who called himself Ágios nor the slight silent boy at her side, who was, or so it seemed, his charge.

Out of the dark came to Mama Straw's ear the plaintive call of a prairie bird. It was a call unlike any she had ever heard before. Texas was a wild and strange land she thought as she looked into the glow of the fire. For a second, she longed for the home she had traveled so far from; from the rough, but known mountains of Tennessee.

Daddy John, like all the Straws, she thought, had always been a dreamer; always looking for what was not known, but simply imagined. Mama Straw reflexively straightened her back and dismissed the notions of where she came from. This woman would protect her man's dream as best she could. And she would see to this new silent one at her side; the one with the strange marks, the strange ways, and a strange protector. Again, the peculiar bird's call floated over the land and filled the darkness.

The little man with the big dreams came into the light of the fire and slowly folded to the ground next to his woman.

"Got the brake fixed on the wagon, Mama," he said. Daddy John reached for the coffee pot on the edge of the fire. "Did you hear that bird out yonder? That's a call I ain't heard fore, how 'bout you, Mama? You heard that one?"

"No. Daddy, I ain't."

Mama Straw was about to get up when she felt the child

next to her relax into her side. She sensed he had fallen asleep, so she remained still and relaxed the tension in her own body. It had been a long day for them both.

"Daddy, when you get up, throw a blanket on us. I think we will rest a bit." Again a faint breath of air caressed her cheek as her heavy eye lids involuntarily closed, and the woman from Tennessee began to snore slightly.

✝

A MARTYR FOR CUSTER

Blood memories

L IEUTENANT ERIN could see the emotion in Major Reno's eyes, and he didn't like what he saw. There was something behind the outward bravado that was belied by the quick shifting of glances in a jerky, reflexive motion. Luke suspected that what he saw clearly was the passion of fear.

Reno's command had its orders from General Custer, and now they moved slowly but steadily along the left bank of Sun Dance Creek toward what their scout had said was the "biggest bunch of Indians," he had ever seen.

Lieutenant Erin was in command of G Company, and he knew that a few miles to the west of their position they would meet the glory of the soldier or the fate of the martyr for the general; the commander who now rode on the other side of the creek, and out of sight of Reno's battalion. Just ahead, sitting almost sideways on his nervous horse, looking behind him more than to the front, Major Reno practically was dancing in the saddle. The commander of G Company, if he had known in advance what was about to happen to him and his men, would have pulled his Colt revolver from its leather holster and shot the major in the head. But fate never offers that view, and just as the lieutenant had done in the village of Chief Black Kettle almost a decade before, he was about to surprise himself by the actions he performed.

All of the officers riding slightly ahead of the column of troopers were riding four abreast in battle formation. Each man slightly raising themselves off the saddle leather and leaning forward to look as far ahead as possible; hoping to get a glimpse of the red devils that would surely be just over the next bluff before they saw them. All expected the command to charge at any moment, and the excitement of the men was exhibited by the horses they rode which pranced about fretfully like they were on parade. Many of the troopers had pulled their revolvers free in anticipation of the looming combat and waved them like flags in the air. All verbal exchanges between the men had now ceased so that the only noise was that of the pounding hooves on the packed hard sand of the banks of Sun Dance Creek.

Lieutenant Erin glanced again across the tributary of the Little Big Horn River, trying to catch sight of General Custer's command, but his battalion was nowhere to be seen. The timber was getting thicker as Reno's troopers approached what they suspected would be Sitting Bull's, Hunkpapa band of Sioux. Erin suddenly felt as if Reno's command was totally alone, and the men he rode with now were to meet their fate apart from the main force of the Seventh Cavalry; a force that had strangely disappeared out of range of sight or sound.

And then Erin heard the command from Major Reno for G Company to fall to the right flank and ride along the timbers to the west. With the troopers now fully positioned for the fight ahead, the pace quickened yet again. All were almost at a gallop as Erin caught sight of what appeared to be about fifty Sioux and Cheyenne warriors, all mounted, riding confidently back in forth in front of the advancing cavalry. The Indian warriors appeared to be deliberately stirring up dust so that their numbers and their positions would be almost impossible to determine. The lieutenant now felt the same intense excitement as he had felt that day nearly eight years before looking down on the Washita River at the sleeping camp of Chief Black Kettle; only this time the Indians were not asleep in their lodges; their ponies painted and their weapons at the ready. He pointed his Colt forward as he anticipated the command to charge from the Major.

But what the lieutenant heard instead at first didn't seem possible, more like a fantastic dream; unreal, a surrealistic utterance from someone or something that never could exist; certainly not from an officer of General George Armstrong Custer' Seventh Cavalry.

"Battalion halt," Reno shouted.

And then the lieutenant heard the same order again, the implausible command being relayed down the line of advancing troopers. Erin only slightly restrained his horse while he held up his revolver to signal to his company to do the same.

"Prepare to fight on foot," came the second improbable order from the major, and as it did, Lieutenant Erin could see all of Reno's command dismount and begin to form picket lines to his left. Just as the lieutenant swung from the saddle, two run-away horses with panicked troopers on their backs came busting through the ranks. Erin recognized Private Runnels, and he thought the second trooper to be O'Hare from A Company but wasn't sure.

The horses had done what all cavalry men dreaded; the powerful jaws of the horses had the bit between their teeth, and there would be no turning the animals by human will or strength; only the fate of a battlefield would do that now.

Lieutenant Erin screamed "Hold your fire," to his troopers, all now prone in the dust and spread at some five-yard intervals just to the left of Sun Dance Creek. The men watched as the two stampeding cavalry horses with helpless riders bobbing like fishing corks on water approached the thick dust that separated the troopers and the swirling mass of Indian warriors about a quarter of a mile to the northwest.

Then the two hapless soldiers disappeared into the earthly cloud that, the lieutenant thought, would surely transform into the fires of hell. For a long moment all was silent. It was if God had called a time-out. The men waited with their rifles at the ready and their horses picketed just behind them. Erin looked around for his commander, but Reno was missing from the ranks. He looked back towards the Indians' position; and, as he did, he heard the firing, first one shot and then another. Then, as if all hell had indeed come to be just ahead of all of Reno's battalion, volley after volley exploded from the swirling cloud. The troopers aimed their Springfield rifles in the direction of the unseen mayhem and waited.

"Hold your fire men," Lieutenant Erin again shouted. "Damn it, hold your fire, our men are in that dust."

Just as he spoke the cloud was parted by a single soldier, on foot, running straight for the troopers of G Company's position. He wore no hat but it was clear it was Private Runnels. The trooper was running as if drunk, swaying first to one side and then the other. Erin prayed that none of his nervous riflemen would mistakenly shoot at the man now trying desperately to return to his comrades. Again the lieutenant screamed, "He's ours boys, let him come, let him come, nobody fire!"

Just as he spoke the command, two Indian braves came into view and were bearing down on the running soldier. The brave in the lead sent first one arrow and then another toward the fleeing trooper. Both missed. The second fired from his rifle and the round caught the private in the left shoulder and spun him around to face the direction from which he was so frantically bolting. That's when the third arrow passed almost completely through the man's throat as all in the battalion watched.

Private Runnels seemed to pause and straighten his stance before he fell like a statue backwards. As his body hit the ground, another dry dust cloud puffed all around his form, sending what looked to be his ghost skyward. The two Indian braves pulled their painted ponies around to present a proud sideways picture to all the cavalry men, most prone, a few officers standing. The one with the rifle raised it, and both the Indians screamed in triumph and spun their horses in their jubilance.

With that taunt, the emotions along the picket lines broke

like a cracked dam. In perfect unison every rifle discharged. The roar was if the god of thunder himself had issued the command to fire. The cloud of dust that had obscured the enemy moments before was likewise duplicated by the cloud of rifle smoke that covered the troopers of Company G. Only the body of the lone private caught between the opposing forces, which now lay like a mannequin on his back, had a clear view of the sky. But his blue eyes were unnaturally wide open, and did not perceive the bright, intense sun that stared back at him. It was swelteringly hot on Sun Dance Creek at three-thirty on the afternoon of June 25th, 1876. Whatever those spiritless eyes did see would be seen by many more of the troopers of the Seventh Cavalry before the day was to fade into darkness.

✝

PEELING THE ONION

The dark timbers

UNABLE TO SEE, the troopers heard what seemed like the sounds of a thousand specters descending on them from the direction of the Sioux and Cheyenne lodges. Lieutenant Erin watched the disintegration of Major Reno's battalion with first disbelief, and then anger as he shouted to all within earshot to re-form their ranks; to do their duty. He again searched for the commander, but realized that he was now the commander. Reno had disappeared from what remained of the formation.

Panic is like a plague. It first touches a very few and demonstrates its intent, and then it touches a few more to demonstrate its inexorable will. Then finally, having peeled away the outer layers of the onion, it goes to the core and does the real work; it demonstrates its overwhelming power over man; over both the best and the worst of men.

As the rifle smoke from the collective volley began to dissipate, Lieutenant Erin stood with what was left of the troopers of his G Company. Along with the seven soldiers that stood with him was the scout Pascal Monroe; the one they called Bean. The tall and skinny prairie ruffian with bright blue eyes that stared a hole through those he chose to look at, but seldom did, now made eye contact with the desperate lieutenant.

"I believe it's time to make it to those timbers, Lieutenant," he said with a calm that was in stark contrast to the chaos that was now fast approaching the remnants of the battalion.

Erin didn't need but a second to evaluate the scout's suggestion and shouted for his men, the few he had still under his command, to move out. He pointed the direction with his Colt as they all mounted and moved obliquely toward what was the only apparent defensible position that could be reached before the mass of painted warriors would overrun their position. Several of the troopers took wild pot shots over their shoulders as they spurred their mounts towards what they hoped would be a defensible refuge. The horses splashed through a shallow creek and all entered the thick timber. Immediately the men set about picketing the mounts and looking for any breastworks they could find for cover.

"They'll likely come at us four or five at a time, Lieutenant, using the trees as cover," Bean said. "It's going to be kind of hot in the woods for a while I suspect."

"Speaking of hot, where in the hottest hell did that major go?" Lieutenant Erin spoke to himself, but the sentiment of anger was loud enough for the scout to hear.

"He went where all deep cowards go that get spooked, I reckon. He went to higher ground." Bean pointed through a break in the trees.

Erin, looking where Bean suggested, clearly could see what the scout meant. Just across the river, the men now hunkered down in the timber could spy their once comrades-in-arms in groups of two's and three's climbing clumsily and frantically up a steep bluff toward what must have appeared as sanctuary. Among the terrified and leaderless climbers, the troopers down below could also see the spikes of dust and rock being kicked up around the soldiers. With regularity, one or the other would drop from the face of bluff and fall back toward the river. But there, they would find no relief in the cool waters on this hot summer day. The river would seal their fate. A final fate brought about by swarms of painted men; men who would slowly kill and mutilate their long-time enemy.

As Erin and Bean watched the slaughter in the distance, they quickly realized the great number of warriors, like a swarm of disturbed bees; had by-passed their defensible position in the timbers and pursued instead the easier prize of troopers fleeing in panicked confusion. There was little to do for Erin and his men but wait, and to prepare to defend their position. Where was Custer? The lieutenant thought. If the remnants of G Company and the terror struck battalion of Reno were to survive the day's battle, Erin knew it would be Custer who would deliver them.

✝

SACRED ARROWS

Revenge has a messenger

SITTING WITH BEARS helped the aged Inkpaduta across the river before he gathered his bow and quiver; the sounds of battle reaching his ears from multiple directions. The old chief called out to the young warrior. Sitting With Bears was anxious to ride out to the fight; it would be his first. But showing regard for this old war chief, he waited. The ancient one, now almost blind, and crippled, shuffled toward the waiting fighter and handed him what would be, the young warrior knew, a sacred arrow.

"Take this, you will need its spirit in the battle you soon must fight," Inkpaduta said in a voice filled with strength, but yet sounding feeble.

Sitting With Bears grasped the shaft of the brightly painted arrow, but as he attempted to retrieve it, Inkpaduta held onto the arrow for a moment. It was as if the old man wanted to take it himself and confront another enemy of his people and his way of life. Finally, as he released his grip on the missile, he peered determinedly at the young warrior and nodded with what appeared to be a smile. It was a much more fatigued look that the old warrior now gave to his young charge than he had but a few years before when the ragged and lost boy came into his camp on the Rosebud River. Then Inkpaduta was still of a fighting spirit; he was still a proud war chief among the Sioux; a war chief that recognized the pain in the young Cheyenne boy's eyes. It was the pain of loss, a pain that all the Sioux had known since the coming of the white man.

It was Inkpaduta that had renamed the young refugee Sitting With Bears and found a place for him in his lodge. The boy was among a few survivors that had made their way north after their village along the Washita River in the Indian territories had been destroyed by many of the same soldiers that now threatened the Sioux and Cheyenne on the Little Bighorn. But this time, Sitting With Bears was no longer afraid and lonely, he was a sinewy and strong brave about to have his chance at revenge. Sitting With Bears shrill war scream echoed off the surrounding bluffs as he flew with the wings of the eagle onto the back of his fresh war pony.

As the young rider and his horse kicked up the dust of departure, the old warrior disappeared in the shroud left behind. Sitting With Bears could feel the power of the beast between his legs. He sensed the horse was as anxious as he to meet the *wasichus,* the evil white invader who sought to take from him all that he had; all that was dear to his people, for a second time.

Quickly he glanced back at the stand of lodges, but almost all behind him was obscured. There was only one place to be now. Sitting With Bears wrapped his legs tightly around the frame of the powerful animal under him. He could see the smoke of battle ahead, most of it coming from the river. He kicked his heels harshly into the sides of his mount, which responded with a wild jump ahead. The warrior yelped like a wolf as he rode to his destiny.

He could also see the battle raging on the bluffs just south of the lodges. That was where he would join the fray. But as he crossed a small clearing, his horse suddenly checked its harsh run and spooked at something lying just ahead on the ground. Sitting With Bears could see it was a trooper, dressed in the blue but covered with white chalk and dust. One arm was extended towards the sky as if in appeal to the gods. His pony veered around the lifeless form and, as it did, he could see that the crows had already feasted on the soft flesh of the eyes.

A shrill war whoop came from his mouth and he again prodded the sides of his horse. As he did, the warrior caught a glimpse of a flash of light being reflected from the timber just ahead. He checked his horse and sat rigid. Sitting With Bears focused his stare on the woods.

He saw the flash again. There were soldiers in the timber. Slowly the warrior dismounted, and crossed the shallow creek that fed into the Little Bighorn River; he crouched low as he moved into the fringes of the trees. His horse began to graze calmly behind him. If he could only find them without being seen, he would have what he sought. The bow he grasped would be his peoples' answer to the death of Black Kettle. The sacred arrow of Inkpaduta would convey the message.

✝

PASCAL'S WAGER

A fool's bet

WITHIN THE SHELTER of the timber and with the battle raging elsewhere, Lieutenant Erin and the scout Bean used the same tree to rest their backs. A couple of troopers nearby were busily trying to pry swollen and spent cartridges from the chambers of their Springfield rifles. Erin could see Corporal Jansen anxiously glancing his way and then back in the direction where the nervous Swede knew his comrades were dying, dying quickly if they were lucky, at the hands of the Sioux and the Cheyenne Dog Soldiers.

"What do you think our chances are of getting back across the river and finding Custer?" Lieutenant Erin spoke in the direction of the scout close on his right side. Without waiting for a response, he asked again, "What do you think are our chances of getting out of this mess we're in? Of leaving these timbers with our hair in its proper place?"

Erin then waited, but there was no answer. At first he

thought the scout hadn't heard him, and then he decided he wouldn't pursue the question; it was rhetorical anyway. They would or they wouldn't; just a matter of fickle fate.

"God willing," the belated answer came from Bean.

When the lieutenant heard the invocation to the mercy of God, he couldn't help but think of his own father; the father who, too, seemed to defer to his God when things were difficult. Luke had grown to hate that answer; that non-answer he called it. Sitting now, his back against a tree, ten rifle rounds in his side pack and four in his Colt revolver, and the world full of hostiles who wanted only to see his innards spilled along the Little Bighorn River; Lieutenant Erin, without turning to face the scout, spoke to Bean with sarcasm.

"Well, you want to turn on the charm then, and ask your God for a little help? I damn well suspect we're going to need some; don't you?"

As if to add emphasis to the lieutenant's words, the crack of a rifle shot sounded nearby, somewhere in the close woods where the soldiers had taken refuge. All the troopers jolted to attention, and waited with rifles raised to ready.

"It's your God, too, Lieutenant," Bean said, declining to recognize either the irreverent question or the threat of the rifle shot. Then he added quietly, "Well, I guess if we don't come out of these woods or out of this battlefield, I'm ready for what's to come."

"What's next? What the hell does that mean?"

"Lieutenant, I think you know what it means."

Erin pulled himself up to a squat and pivoted to face the scout. He forced a broad smile.

"You poor scalawag, you still believe in all that mumbo

jumbo, don't you? That heaven and hell stuff? I'd of thought a man like you, out here among all this savagery, would have given that notion up long ago."

The scout, likewise, pivoted to his feet, but stood full up, and before again leaning against the tree; he surveyed as best he could around his position.

"Yeah, I do. And, no I haven't. I'm ready if my end comes here; here in these timbers."

"Bean, let me tell you what your big reward is going to be. You're going to pass into the land of dark, that's it, scout. The big black. The same hole all these savages fall into. The same one I fall into, and the same one that my pious father slipped into without a kind word from anyone. That's what you get for all your trouble of calling out to your God. But, you know what, you won't know the difference, that's what I think is so damn ironic about it; no, not so much ironic as tragic. What a waste of time. You best be putting your faith in the knife on your belt and that army issued Colt in its scabbard. That's your savior if Custer doesn't show, if you're going to have one this day, scout."

Erin, having made his speech, started away from the tree toward the corporal's position, but Bean reached out and caught Erin by the sleeve. He had hesitated to offer a rebuttal, but then spoke.

"Lieutenant, I know you don't want to hear any sermon, and I won't give you one. But let me put this on your plate to chew on."

"Scout, we don't have time for this debate now, wouldn't you agree?"

"Maybe this is the only thing we really have time for, sir. You had your say, give me mine."

Lieutenant Erin nodded and turned toward Bean.

"Let's say that this mess we've gotten ourselves into doesn't turn out well for either one of us. Let's say we both get it right now, together. Let's say we face death in lockstep. You buy that part?"

"Well, argument aside, I reckon that's the one real possibility right now," Erin again smiled but with more a countenance of mockery than humor.

"Okay, here it is. I tell you I'm ready to come face-to-face with my God. In fact, I can say that I'm kind of looking forward to it. You know, finding out after all this time."

Erin lifted his eyebrows slightly and shook his head slowly.

"And you say that what I'm going to get is nothing but black. This is it. There's nothing after this. All that's gone before is not prologue but final epilogue; no, not even epilogue. Just nothing. That's your point?"

"Pretty simple isn't it, Bean? I think you would have to agree."

"Yeah, Lieutenant, pretty simple. But let's suppose, just as I said before, we die right here and right now. One moment we exist, the next we don't. The stuff in these bodies immediately starts the journey to soup or dust or whatever."

Bean paused as the sounds of rifle fire again became more intense and seemed to be moving along the river toward their cover in the timbers.

"Now, if you are right, nothing but black, if this is right; then guess what, you will never know, and neither will I. And, you know what, this is your irony for you; you will never get to say 'I told you so' now will you?"

Erin started to respond, but the scout cut him off.

"But...but, what if I am right, Lieutenant? What if rather than your no color ending, your fade to black, we suddenly find ourselves sitting in the midst of the most brilliant light of all colors imaginable. This entire scene that we're playing out right now is over; it is over like it never happened. All that was our lives, our hopes, our concerns, everything is no more. And, none of it is even in memory. There is nothing else but what we face at this first moment of timeless, spaceless death."

Bean finally paused and waited for Erin to say something, but the officer was silent.

Bean continued, "So, in that first moment or whatever it is, we see that we are sitting side-by-side in front of, guess who? Yeah, Lieutenant, sitting face-to-face with your father's creator; with his God. If that be the case; if I'm the one who is right after all. If all my mumbo jumbo, as you call it, was suddenly right there, and as real as I am now. Well, which one of us would you want to be?"

Erin looked intensely at the scout for a long moment. Finally he said, "But you're not, Bean. That's just it; you're not."

As the scout pulled his Colt from its holster and took a step that began to separate the two soldiers, he said, "Sounds like a fool's bet to me, Lieutenant. But, like I said, I'm ready." It was the scout's turn to offer a slight smile to his lieutenant.

Lieutenant Erin returned Bean's look with a quizzical stare.

"Never knew you were such a philosophic type, scout."

Lieutenant Erin turned away from Bean, and moved away from the tree toward the position of his corporal. He had taken a couple of quick steps when the brightly painted arrow entered his eye socket. The steel tipped shaft surgically separated the soft, communicative tissue between the two hemispheric lobes of Lieutenant Luke Erin's brain and cut the spinal cord at the base of the neck before the point exited flesh and reflected softly the dappled light of the woods. The lieutenant opened his mouth as if to acknowledge the injury, but he said nothing as his crumpling body first folded against the tree, and then slumped toward the ground. Before Erin's head hit the soft soil of the woods he was caught by the army scout, who could now hear clearly a battle scream coming somewhere from the thick timbers surrounding the few huddled troopers.

Bean looked at the lifeless soldier in his arms and whispered a simple call to his maker on the dead man's behalf. With that, he lowered the form to the ground and cocked the hammer on his rifle and waited for the gruesome faces he expected to appear from the shadows.

He was ready for what was to come.

✝

PLAYING IN THE DEVIL'S GARDEN

Black tulips in Texas

THE RIGHT REVEREND Ducus Butcher stung the rump of his horse with the tip of his whip. The insulted animal moved along at the same pace as before but snorted its disapproval at the unwarranted hurt. The buggy rattled its way up the long, straight set of ruts in the dirt towards the farm house in the distance. As the reverend approached closer he already knew much about the Straw family; not by acquaintance, he was new to this vast and wild land, but by the appearance of all he surveyed before him. The splendid order of what he saw assured the man dressed in black that these were his people. He was anxious to take them into his flock; to bring them to his side and within his guidance. He again smarted the poor horse that transported him, and again the creature only snorted.

Reverend Butcher knew something else about the Straws. He knew that they had that boy. That boy, near to being a man, that never speaks people said. The stories told of the boy had reached his ears nearly a year before, but this was to be his first face-to-face with the one all the God fearing on these prairies said was haunted with the demons. Demons indeed, what a wonderful prospect he thought as he could just make out the large woman who stood square and erect on the long porch of the house. The reverend knew surely that this must be the one called Mama Straw. He smiled only slightly for he didn't want to display his enthusiasm for the task at hand. He didn't want to betray his intent too quickly.

As the man of the Book drew within hailing distance he could see the big woman turn obliquely and issue some command or other to those inside the native stone house with real glass windows. Directly, two other family members exited the dwelling and aligned themselves on either side of the matriarch. The reverend was sure that the lean short man to her right was John Straw, but the very tall man to her left he didn't know of. He did know that, for some unsettling notion, he didn't like the looks of this one. He hoped that this stranger would not prove a hindrance to his plans.

The reverend was also hoping that the mysterious, mute lad would make his appearance; but as he reigned in his weary horse with a cruel jerk, there was no sign of the boy. Ducus Butcher displayed a grin showing perfect white teeth to the Straws as he practically jumped from the seat of the buggy and started for the porch.

Mama Straw only nodded slightly towards the bounding reverend, which was a sign for her husband to step forward and extend his hand in greeting. After the greeting between the two, Daddy John stepped back into formation without another word. Mama Straw then spoke.

"Reverend Butcher, the Straws welcome you to our home. We were told of your approaching visit by a traveling merchant last week. Come join us." Her greeting was lacking enthusiasm Butcher thought, and he sensed a bit of sternness in the woman's voice that he wasn't sure he liked to hear. He responded only with an overly cheerful thank you, as he anticipated an introduction to the tall stranger that didn't bother to look his way. But Mama Straw disappointed him a second time, and simply motioned that they take a seat in the rockers that occupied most of the porch.

As all settled in their chairs, the tall stranger moved quietly off the porch and passed out of sight along the side of the house.

"Madam, if you will excuse my curiosity," the reverend shifted his seat to look in the direction where the stranger had stood, "the tall gentleman, a family member perhaps?"

Mama Straw didn't immediately respond, but finally said only, "A man who works for us," the woman's truncated answer suggested that was to be all she had to say about the man.

"Oh, I see. Well, rather a tall fellow I would say, with quite a mysterious demeanor he is." Butcher adjusted perceptively and shifted his rocker back to its original position. "But, be that as it may, let me begin our visit by revealing its most pious purpose. And, so properly, maybe it would wise to offer a prayer to our Lord."

Before the reverend could begin, the door covered with a fine screen creaked as it opened slowly, and thus demanded the attention in its direction. Daddy John called out to the string-bean figure standing halfway through the portal. "Come out, Little Jack, come on, we have company. Come out and show yourself, boy!"

Again Reverend Butcher shifted his rocker to take fully into view the new arrival. "And this would be the one I have heard so much about; the mute one," Butcher said as he came to his feet. As he did the boy withdrew slightly back into the house, partially obscuring his features in the shadows of the doorway.

"Come on out, Little Jack," Mama Straw said in a voice both stern and soft. At that familiar assurance, Little Jack took a step onto the broad porch and cleared the doorway.

"How old are you now, my boy?" Butcher asked before he thought, but then he corrected himself. He redirected his question to Mama Straw. "The boy, I think is almost a man by the looks of him, am I correct?"

"Yes, as near as we know he is near to seventeen or eighteen years," she answered.

"Well, madam, I was about to tell you why I have come to your home; and now, with the lad standing right before me, I will be pointed," Butcher slid slowly back into his seat and faced squarely his hosts. "He is the primary purpose of this visit. More correctly it is his salvation that has brought me to you today."

Without recognizing what she was doing, Mama Straw reached her hand into the pocket on the front of her apron and unconsciously fingered the small rock figurine that she always found in the folds. Deep inside of her, deep where understandings that are vague, but real, find their residence, the strong woman felt a shudder pass over her body. The vibration moved through her big frame and down her arm to her fingers. There it was transmitted to the stone. The little stone seemed to warm in her hand, as Mama Straw looked away from the Right Reverend, first to her husband, and then, with a fixed gaze, at Little Jack.

"It is my understanding that the boy, this half-breed, is still to be admitted into God's grace, am I right, madam?"

Mama Straw heard the man's words, but she thought she heard more. She knew she didn't like the way he referred to her son. She hadn't heard that reference to Little Jack's blood since the day they rescued the lad from the banks of the Red River. She remained silent, resisting the politeness of an answer, but continued to finger the amulet in her apron pocket.

The sudden silence was uncomfortable for the reverend so Butcher redirected his attention to Daddy John.

"My dear Mr. Straw you do understand, I can only assume that every day that goes forward this young man is in danger of eternal damnation. The Holy sacrament of baptism is one of the most strident demands of the Scriptures. He must die in the water and receive the Spirit into his soul; he must do so without delay, I assure you!"

Daddy John only nodded, and then he looked, as he always did, toward his woman.

"Yes we do, Reverend Butcher," Mama Straw said, not waiting for her husband to answer the reverend. As she did she looked past Butcher, subconsciously trying to see the tall man that had been their silent helper for many years. He should be on this porch, she thought. He should hear these words of this self-proclaimed man of God. He would know what they should really do about such an important thing. But, the giant, blue-eyed man had disappeared.

"Madam, I really must insist, it is my calling to bring such matters of faith and God's love to the fore." Again, the reverend turned, as if to plea to the man on the porch for intervention. This time he was rewarded for his persistence.

"Mama," Daddy John said as he stood up and walked toward her. "Mama, it is time. We must do this for the boy's sake. We can't take the chance with the soul of this lad, one we have protected from all other harm for many years."

Mama Straw didn't look at Daddy John directly, but as she continued to finger the stone, she too stood up and looked strongly at Reverend Butcher.

"Why else have you come here sir?" As she spoke she motioned for Little Jack to join her at her side. The boy, near to being a man, as always without a sound, moved obediently next to the large, strong woman. "There is something else, I feel it, Mr. Butcher," she said.

The reverend immediately made note of the difference in address and now joined the Straws in standing.

"Madam Straw," he said slowly and deliberately, hoping to counter the doubt that had taken hold. "I don't think I understand your question. I have come all this way to your wonderful home because I had been told that you have a boy in your house, one struck with the silence of innocence, one that is in need of the protection of our Lord. Madam, you must understand that this is my calling, my duty, indeed, my purpose in life. I am a servant of our Lord Jesus Christ; and I should add, a servant of His children. This is my only purpose; my only purpose I assure you."

Daddy John suddenly intervened again with a force in his voice that was so unlike him that Mama Straw was startled.

He looked directly to Reverend Butcher, and as he did he drew the arm of Little Jack to him.

"Reverend, we will not hesitate any longer. The soul of

the lad, his salvation, is all that is important now. We want you to cleanse him in the water of our Lord, to wash him in the Blood of the Lamb. That's what we want. Yes sir, that's what we want."

Mama Straw silently sighed, but she said nothing more. She felt Little Jack shift toward her husband, and she didn't make an effort to pull him back.

She let the small rock owl drop to the bottom of her apron pocket and took a step towards the front door. As she did, she once again reflexively looked out toward the barn for Ágios. And then she caught a fleeting glimpse of the tall man as he moved around the corral and entered the woods. Mama Straw could see him headed to the river below the fields to the west. There was an ache in her heart that she knew he could ease if she could only talk to him. This day there was something dreadful about, Mama Straw just didn't know what it was. She knew that the giant would, but all was just moving too quickly.

✝

Little Jack's Resurrection

Speaking in tongues

O NCE MORE Reverend Butcher put the sting of his whip to his horse and the buggy lurched forward. By his side sat Little Jack; as always, quiet and at peace in the place that only he visited and understood. The reverend constrained his horse to a slow trot, and the two moved away from the Straw's farm house and onto the trail that would take them to the waters. The waters that would bring the young silent boy-man into the fold; would let him die to the life he had only known in the sweet and gentle Straw clan, and emerge reborn into another life that only God knew about.

Mama Straw fidgeted anxiously as Daddy John slowly, he did everything at a pace that resembled ice melting, brought the mule from the corral to his small wagon that he used to fetch supplies from the trading post.

"Daddy, can't you hurry up, just this once? They're already nearly to the river I'm sure, and here we sit. I don't want to miss the boy's baptism," Mama Straw pleaded.

"We'll get there," is all Daddy John said as he pulled the chin strap taunt and fidgeted with the stiff leather buckle.

Reverend Butcher directed the buggy to the edge of the river known by all that came this way as Table Rock Crossing. It was a splendid flat rock of limestone that ran, like a natural dam, across the whole width of the watercourse. The smooth surface of the rock offered a stable roadway for wagons making their way across the unpredictable waters of the Brazos. It also held back the cold clean water so that a man could stand with the frigid liquid up to his waist and take comfort in the heat of a Texas summer. The reverend figured it would be a perfect place to perform the task he had in mind; the task he had been given.

"Come on, lad, let's get out of the buggy and move to the waters of redemption," Reverend Butcher stuck the butt end of the buggy whip into a round tube just next to the seat and let himself slowly descend to the ground. He moved to the front of his horse and hobbled the beast.

Little Jack hadn't moved or given any indication that he heard the reverend's command, so Butcher walked slowly back to the buggy seat.

"Did you hear me, boy? Let's move to the river. We have God's work to do in these waters."

Little Jack finally looked at the man, but then he turned to face in the direction of his home. Reverend Butcher reached out his hand to the lad and smiled broadly. Without taking the assistance offered, Little Jack sprang from the buggy seat, his brogan boots stirring the dust as they hit the ground. The boy moved toward the river as if he knew surely what he was expected to do. The reverend followed along, glancing over his shoulder to see if the Straws were coming. There was no sign of them so Butcher quickened his pace to catch up with his charge. The reverend came to his side just as Little Jack took the first steps into the cold, shallow water. Butcher knew he had his chance. He, too, splashed into the water and the two trod side-by-side on the flat stone out several yards from the bank.

"Praise the Lord," shouted Reverend Butcher. "Praise the Lord, indeed," he shouted again. "As John did for Jesus, I shall do for you," his voice rising to a certain shrillness that silenced the soft songs of the wild birds along the river.

With the exhortation, Butcher grabbed hold of Little Jack with both hands, and without encountering any resistance he lowered the boy into the flowing waters of the river, completely submersing his body into the stream. The Right Reverend was silent; he offered no prayer, he said nothing. He forcefully held Little Jack under the water.

The reverend felt the first tugs of the struggle as the boy began to try and free himself from Butcher's powerful grip. With a burst of youthful strength, Little Jack finally broke the surface of the water, but before he could suck in air the reverend's strong hold pushed him back below the surface. Little Jack was drowning.

The reverend never saw the one who grabbed him; he only felt the crush of two great arms around his mid-section as the being behind him lifted the black clad man into the air. Butcher reacted to the power that now had him captured and was forced to let go of Little Jack; his lungs emitted a primal scream in pain. The reverend was suspended aloft for a long moment as if he was a rag doll in the hands of a giant, and then, the captured man came crashing down. The water parted to receive the holy man now just as it had done for Little Jack. But this time, The Right Reverend would not be saved.

Little Jack first spat out the cold liquid that had assaulted his lungs with a fit of coughing; he gasped violently in an effort to fill the vacuum with air. The boy didn't look back at the struggle behind him, but in few extended steps reached the river's edge and cleared the cold water. He bent over at the knees for a moment and breathed deeply again and again. He could hear the sounds of the skirmish behind him. Then he heard a familiar voice command him to run, to run to Mama Straw. "Run, boy, run!" So Little Jack Straw ran.

Suddenly Little Jack stopped, and he slowly turned back to the Table Rock. He saw the giant standing tall, dripping wet, and gazing down the river. Then Little Jack let his gaze shift down the river, and he saw the black form floating on the waters, like a bloated log. As he watched the dark form gain momentum in the stream, his eyes met those of his friend Ágios. Little Jack thought he was about to cough again; but it was not a cough that left his lips but a word. In Cheyenne he spoke his first word.

"Hi vi ssi no ho," was all he said.

Little Jack collapsed to his knees and began to cry softly. He bowed his head and put his head between his trembling hands; he made an attempt to say the word again. It came to his lips easily and he heard himself speak the word. There was a rhythm to it, something about the sound; something about the word itself that he knew was natural to him. He knew what he had said to the giant, what it meant, and he knew why he had said it.

As Little Jack lifted his head and wiped away the tears, he

said the word again, and again he looked on the water for Ágios. But this time the one he had known for so long wasn't there; wasn't to be seen under the bright sun that shown with a luminance that almost blinded. Neither was the floating log; it had moved down the river and was gone. Little Jack came to his feet and looked all around, but the giant was gone too. He was alone. He spoke his one phrase again in a strange and wonderful tongue.

By some unseen grace, Little Jack had learned a language. He at last could tell his story; a story he knew well, a story in his heart. It was the story of his mother, and the story of his mother's people. Little Jack had carried this story with him for all the years he had sat mutely at the side of Mama Straw and Daddy John. It was a story that had been given to him in the womb of his mother. Now he would tell it to the people that had rescued the naked boy in the crate so long ago.

Little Jack, the half-breed, who was the seed that had been planted on the high bluffs of the Washita River, would now scatter it so that there might be redemption in the life of a man he had never known; a man who lived within his spirit.

Little Jack said the Cheyenne words again as his eyes searched for a sign of Ágios.

✝

SEED ON THE WIND

The return of the owl

MAMA STRAW adjusted her frame so as to take up the center of the wagon's seat. "Daddy John, I do swear that if you get any slower you're going to stop altogether."

The old farmer, as usual, seemed to pay no mind to his woman's scolding but simply directed the mule down the well-worn path that would take them to the river.

"That so-called preacher better not baptize that boy before we get there is all I need say." Mama Straw made a show of fidgeting in her seat, crossing her big arms and straightening her back. Daddy John knew what that meant so he swatted the mule none too gently. Daddy John's mule, having through the years learned his master's ways and gate, didn't seem to move any quicker; which was probably just as well. The scene now being played out at the Table Rock Crossing on the river wouldn't have been for this couple's eyes.

As Daddy John, a bit more gently this time, prodded his

mule again, the Cheyenne braves appeared suddenly in their path; they seemed to come out of nowhere. He counted at least ten in front of the wagon, and another half-dozen coming up from the rear and to the sides. In all his time on the frontier of Texas, he and Mama Straw had been spared the terror that these Dog Soldiers wrought with their painted faces and their screams.

In his haste to get to the river, Daddy John had neglected to retrieve his shotgun. But as he watched the encirclement, like a malevolent prairie tornado surround the wagon; he was glad he didn't have the weapon. It would have been of no use. Whatever was to be; if these were the Straws' last moments, it would be up to the Creator, he was sure of that. Daddy John pulled on the reins and the old mule obediently complied. The frontier farmers sat silently and waited for the agitated warriors to do what they would do.

Several of the Indians were already poking around in the bed of the wagon and shouting. What they were saying Daddy John had no idea. He suspected they were after any supplies he might have. Surely, he thought, they wouldn't want his mule, broken as it was.

Then with no warning, one of the braves jumped on the front seat next to Mama Straw. He had his knife out, but he didn't appear ready to use it.

"Food, want food!" he said in a clear voice, demanding but not threatening.

"We have no food here," Mama Straw answered, drawing the attention of warrior.

"Food, where food?" the Indian responded.

"In the house, food in the house," she said and turned slightly to point the way back to the farm house. She knew the Indian didn't understand her.

"Food, want food!" This time the words were louder. Impatient sounds that signaled a change of mood; a change of mood that portended ill. The brave raised his knife, this time in the direction of Daddy John. To the old man's credit he remained calm and still, offering no resistance, no reaction to the threat.

One of the warriors mounted the mule. Most of the others came very close to the wagon. Some lowered their carbines and pointed them at Daddy John. Several let out with loud and sustained cries that made the air around seem like fragile glass that would shatter at any moment. Mama Straw reached out and took Daddy John's hand in hers. The Indian with the knife paid no attention to the gesture; but, instead, with a swift almost imperceptible motion nicked the neck of the wagon's driver. Again he demanded, "Food, want food!"

As a small amount of the old man's blood showed in the wound, and as Mama Straw instinctively reached out to stop the bleeding, she then heard the voice call out. She didn't understand the words, they were of the same language as the Indians that surrounded the helpless pair, but she knew, somehow, that whoever said the words was not one of them. And then, as if she was in a dream, Mama Straw saw who had shouted at the threatening raiders. Everything that now threatened her and Daddy John was no longer important. No matter what would happen, Mama Straw felt as if she was witnessing a miracle. She was in the presence of God's Grace. She was sure of it.

It was Little Jack approaching, shouting, not in fear, but in a voice that seemed to stun the warriors as much as it did Mama Straw. Little Jack came among them with confidence, almost a swagger, that the woman could not imagine from this gentle, silent boy she had known for all their years in Texas. She reflexively called out to him; and he looked her way for an instant, but he didn't respond. And whatever he said to the warriors, Mama Straw and Daddy John had no idea; but whatever he said, they listened to.

The brave, who had a moment before been so threatening, bounded from the wagon; and in single powerful motion, remounted his painted pony. Many of the others, too, moved away from the wagon. They now surrounded Little Jack. The young man spoke in their language. He waved his arms about for emphasis, and all the braves listened. Some shouted, not at him, Mama Straw could clearly see, but with him. To the woman it was if the boy had never been theirs. As if he had only floated among them as a ghost floats among the living; occasionally sensed but never heard.

Now Little Jack with a motion of strength flew up behind the warrior who the old couple figured was the leader. He took his seat on the war horse like he was born on that animal. Without command all the Dog Soldiers formed around Little Jack. Mama Straw knew they were about to leave. She couldn't help herself; she began to weep quietly. The warrior, with Little Jack behind, rode close to the woman. Her son reached out his hand, and Mama Straw understood what he wanted. She brought it out of her apron and extended it towards the one she had known for so long, but not known at all.

The stone owl, warm to the touch, dropped into Little Jack's hand. He nodded toward Mama Straw, with what was not quite a smile. He said something in the Indian tongue to her. She didn't understand the words, but she understood the stare that came from those deep green eyes; those mystical eyes that must have seen into her soul at that moment. She also noticed once again, as she had so many times before, the strange mark on his head. It was a brilliant and deep red now; deeper than she had ever seen.

Then the shouts of the warriors shocked her back into the moment, and she watched as the band galloped away. Daddy John and Mama Straw sat there, not moving, on the seat of their wagon. The old mule, as always, patiently waited for his instructions.

✝

SLEEPING IN THE PROMISED LAND

Stone birds can fly away

DADDY JOHN and Mama Straw sat side-by-side in a pair of well-worn rockers on the porch. As they did most things these days, their rocking motion was in unspoiled harmony. Each, too, without being obvious to the other, peered out across their farm with eyes that were both searching and sad. Without understanding what they were searching for; they unconsciously hoped to catch sight of Ágios or Little Jack walking together on their way home. But, of course, the old frontier couple never did. The two had vanished, after many years together, in only a moment.

Every now and then Mama Straw had the strange notion that maybe the two never had really existed. But those thoughts faded as quickly as they came, and the matriarch knew that the aching in her heart for her little saint and the giant that protected him was real. She knew that the stone owl, which without thinking she reflexively probed for in her apron pocket but no longer could be found, too, was real. And she knew that Little Jack was blessed by the Grace of God; was somehow in His service wherever he was.

As she moved gently back and forth, she turned her gaze toward Daddy John who was now asleep, his unkept whiskered chin was pressed hard into his chest, but still he rhythmically rocked in his chair. Mama Straw loved her dear man from Tennessee. As she watched him, she softly voiced a prayer that God would help her keep him safe in his Promised Land.

Mama Straw once again gazed out onto the land hoping to see a familiar figure in the distance; there was none.

✝

End of Part One

EPILOGUE TO PART ONE

God's Loafers

Neither here
Nor there

L UKE FOLLOWED the crooked path and was surrounded by lush, green foliage that smelled like fresh-baked cinnamon bread; an aroma he remembered from Grandma Thornton's kitchen. It seemed to float all around him like a sweet cloud, and he began to sense that the fragrance, strangely, was being emitted from his own body.

The faint songs of birds drifted, like the scent, on the air. He strained to listen to the soft sounds as he lengthened his stride in anticipation, of what he had no idea. Just ahead he could see his route veered sharply first to the left and then just as abruptly back to the right. Luke wondered why he felt anxious. He reached the first turn and took it, and as he did everything that his senses recognized changed, transforming bit-by-bit with each step he took. As he turned to the right, the saturated colors that had enveloped him; the greens, the deep yellows, the brilliant blues, began to fade, first into a pale version of themselves, and then into a transparent glow with little color at all. Finally, all about him was whiteness like no other he had ever witnessed.

He advanced deeper into the strangeness, and then noticed what appeared to be a white raven promenading proudly directly in his path. The bird was difficult to see; the white on white revealed only indistinct hints of movement, the creature was more a ghostly shadow than substance.

Just beyond the bird, Luke then noticed a small, pine folding chair which appeared to be resting on nothing at all. He approached it slowly. As he reached the hanging chair, Luke stood beside it and waited. For what, he wasn't sure. He didn't have to wait long for, as if from the fog, a man was suddenly directly in front of him.

The figure was dressed rather sloppily Luke thought. He didn't want to have such thoughts, but he couldn't help himself. The man's shirt, colorful as it was, stood out in a dramatic contrast to the brilliant, almost blinding, white all around. The shirt wasn't particularly tidy or, for that matter, even attractive. There appeared to be a loose thread descending from the collar, and Luke resisted the urge to reach out and pluck the errant string from the shirt. The man's trousers were of shiny corduroy; at one time they must have been a dark grey, when they were new, Luke thought. On his feet he wore scuffed and disfigured loafers without socks. And, for some unsounded reason, Luke had the distinct notion that he had seen this disheveled fellow before. He stood waiting for something to happen; for the man to speak.

"Sit down. Go ahead, young man, make yourself comfortable."

The voice was so deep and resonant that the sound of it jolted Luke; but, at the same instant, it sounded so familiar. Startled, Luke eased down onto the seat of the chair as instructed. Consciously he tried not to look around and instead kept his focus on the man in the bright colored shirt. As he did, a small bird, Luke thought it a wren, fluttered to perch on his knee. The bird twittered and flipped its small upright tail to-and-fro in a determined rhythm. Luke resisted the urge to shoo it away; the active small bird made him even more nervous. He couldn't help himself, he was afraid the feathered animal might poop on his leg right in front of this stranger.

"Ágios tells me you're a bit uncomfortable here," the man said in a voice that was both musical and strong. "Luke, do you know where you are?"

Abruptly, Luke felt like crying but resisted the urge. He opened his mouth to answer the question, but no words would come. So he closed his eyes and clenched his teeth hard trying to find a space where he could collect himself. He felt naked, absolutely exposed. He desperately wanted to answer the question, but any words he could think of seemed to him to be so out-of-place here. Nothing worked for Luke; sitting on the small chair, facing this man. All the cleverness he had always thought he had, now had evaporated like mist on a summer morning.

"Really, Luke, you don't have to fear anything here. You are beyond the dominion of fear. Why you still retain those feelings and emotions are solely in your will. They are notions you have brought with you like unnecessary baggage. Don't worry, son, it's not uncommon; especially for those that have never really taken this place seriously."

The man in the colored shirt pointed at the small bird, and it fluttered up to Luke's shoulder and began to sing softly. Luke couldn't help himself, and he giggled as the sound of the bird's pleasant song penetrated deeply into his awareness. The man smiled. Luke tried not to react, to retain a detached composure, but in spite of himself he smiled in return.

Peace flooded though him as if the dam had not so much broken, but just wasn't there anymore. He felt the gentle water flow over and through him; and suddenly he became aware of his soul. His spirit, what Luke had always been, was now clear. Every complicated notion of his existence, every twist and turn and doubling back now was no more. All he heard was the song of that little bird, and it was the sound of simple, overwhelming joy and love; the joy of knowing without trying to know.

"So, Luke, what would you like to say to me?"

Luke's shoulders slumped slightly as he tried again to speak. The wren offered another short song that seemed to help him. It gave Luke just enough courage that he was able to utter, softly, inaudibly one word.

"Ashamed." he said finally more forcefully but still with a softness of voice that Luke had never heard himself use before. Suddenly he again felt panic, and stood up in a reflexive jerk. He thought of running back down the path that had brought him to this place, but when he turned to look for it, it was not there.

"It's all right," the man said. "I understand. You've come home. That shame, like the other worldly notions you've brought, can, too, be left behind."

Luke submissively slumped back down into his seat and attempted to hide his face in his hands. When he finally found the composure to lift his face, the disheveled man was no longer seated in front of him. Everything had changed again; only the little bird was still on his knee. Luke made an effort to stand, but he couldn't. His thoughts raced ahead, and he was more confused than ever.

"Hello, Luke, you can call me Ágios if you wish. I suspect you might have a question or two." The voice, too, was very familiar. Luke couldn't place it, but he knew he had heard before. When he turned to face the source he saw who it was.

Luke stared at the man but hesitated to call out his name, instead he blurted, "Where did he go?" As he searched, his eyes moved rapidly from left to right. "Are you, are you…?"

"As I said, Ágios is the name." As he spoke, the man mysteriously produced another small chair and sat down; he leaned back slightly and smiled.

"No, but you can say I work for Him. The one in the colorful shirt has asked me to help you with your transition. He understands that you are struggling."

"You mean…"

"Yes, God wants you to do what you have never done before, Luke. He wants you to make a choice, and He is willing to grant your wish; if that is what you choose."

The man stood up and motioned for Luke to do the same. Luke hesitated, he wasn't sure he could stand. But his body reacted dutifully to the instruction, and he solidly came to his feet. The man came alongside and pointed into the distance.

"Luke, do you see that?" He motioned with his head in the direction he wanted Luke to look. Luke obeyed the instruction.

After a short while of staring into the whiteness, he reluctantly turned to face Ágios. "No, no I don't think I do. What am I supposed to be looking at?" Luke tried again to focus his gaze in the direction that had been pointed out to him, but still he could only see white.

The man smiled slightly. "Oh, I'm sorry. Now look, do you see anything yet?"

And there they were. Directly in front of Luke, stood two massive doors standing alone with no apparent structure to support them. One was opened to the right, and the other was opened to the left. Through the one to the left, Luke could see a brilliant emerald color with patches of blue and fluffy swirls of misty white all around the edges. The opened door on the right was filled only with a consistent tone of silver.

"Yes, I see it, there're two doors," Luke said excitedly, "Yes, I see them now. Two doors, right?"

"Yes, I'm happy you see them clearly. You have made a wish in front of God, and He knows your heart. He understands you, Luke. You can have that wish if you so want it." At that, Ágios stepped back from the doors, and Luke mechanically stepped back with him.

"I don't think I understand. I didn't wish for anything. All I said was 'ashamed,' that's all I could say."

"Oh but you did, Luke. It was a wish so strong that God couldn't, or should I say more precisely, wouldn't ignore it. This is not how things are normally done around here, but there is something very special about your wish. You may have it, as I said, if you so decide."

Luke stood as still as an old tree in the forest, but try as he might, he couldn't understand what it was that he had wished. Finally he turned to face the man, but now he too had vanished. Luke stood alone before the two doors that gave no hint as to where they led.

And then, without a sound or warning, Luke became aware of a soft, almost imperceptible presence on his shoulder. The once earth-bound man, now standing in a place like no other, cautiously turned his head; and there again he saw the small, insignificant bird. She was singing in the loveliest way, her erect feathered tail dancing all about like a merry piper. Tones that were clear and melodic, danced and conveyed everything that Luke needed to know about what he was to do. He shivered so strongly that he felt that whatever form he had in this place would dissolve into nothing, dissolve and join the veil of mist that enshrouded him.

Then, without hesitation, Luke stepped through the portal on the left. He had done as God had wanted; he had finally made the choice.

The small wren, left behind and without a perch, took flight and fluttered away on wings as quiet as a butterfly.

✝

PART TWO

BLOOD FEATHER

Justice has God's sanction,
Revenge only man's

THE OATH OF THE JADE OWL

Memories in the blood

"I'm drowning in the river of my great father's blood. The crimson waters of injustice wash over me and stain my memories. I cannot breathe. I must right the wrong that was done in those days long ago. But I cannot reach those who did this thing, so I will reach those who glory in the tale. I will take their spirit and mix it with the water and watch as it flows to the sea. And there, it will at last mix with the spirit of my great father, finally together in justice for all eternity.

The Oath of the Jade Owl, sons of the Cheyenne

SEND A WHITE RAVEN

A long time coming

FATHER JUAN walked slowly to the open office door as he looked at his appointment list. His next meeting both intrigued and surprised the priest. He thought he recognized the name but wasn't sure.

"Deborah," he called out without looking up. "My next appointment, is that who I think it is?"

The parish secretary called back, "What did you say, Father Juan?"

"My two o'clock; my calendar says it's a Seth Ironwood. Isn't that the sheriff of Custer County?" The father finally looked up and walked into the hall from where he could see Debbie. "Is someone in the parish in trouble?" he added.

"The answer to the first question is yes. As for the second, Father Juan, I don't know. I can tell you that when he called he didn't mention a specific reason for the visit. The sheriff only said he wanted to talk to a priest." Debbie stood up and came around to the front of her desk.

"Umm!" Father Juan said softly and turned back to his office.

"Father Juan," Debbie called to him, "I guess you will know soon enough. Sheriff Ironwood just drove into the parking lot."

"Okay, send him in as soon as he comes in the office."

Debbie displayed a broad and welcoming smile as Sheriff Ironwood opened the door to the parish office. She noted a couple of things immediately. One, how tall and stock-straight the man was. And two, as he approached her desk and smiled, she was taken by his eyes. Taken by how bright and deep they appeared for such an old man. The blue color projected from the sheriff's face like beacons. The secretary couldn't stop staring at his eyes.

"Hello, I'm...."

"Sheriff Ironwood," Debbie interrupted.

"That's right. I'm here to see the father. I have a two o'clock."

"Yes, Sheriff...."

"Seth." Please just call me Seth."

"Sure, Sheriff. I mean Seth. Father Juan is expecting you. His office is right over there." Debbie pointed down the short hall. As she did the father appeared and approached his guest with his hand extended.

"Good afternoon, Sheriff, I'm Father Juan Bosco. I know you by your excellent reputation, but, if I'm not mistaken, we've never met. Correct?"

"No, Father, I don't think we have." Seth looked a bit uneasy so the priest invited him to join him in his office and led the way. The father pointed to the short couch just inside the door and the sheriff sat down. Father Juan pulled a chair on casters just opposite the sheriff and sat down as well.

"Well, Mr. Ironwood, I must tell you that I'm a bit surprised by your visit. To be truthful, I'm hoping you're not here on official business. Don't like to see any of my parishioners in trouble." The father leaned slightly forward and rested his elbows on his knees.

"No. And please, I hope you will call me Seth. There's nothing official about this visit. It is very personal, I assure you."

"Of course, Seth it is then. Well that's good to hear; I mean about it not being an official visit."

Father Juan leaned back in his chair and paused for a moment. "So, Seth, what can I do for you today?"

Ironwood hesitated. He was usually the one in control; the one asking the questions. As was his habit, he looked first up at the ceiling and then around the room. There were books on three long shelves, a few mementos scattered here and there about the room in no immediately recognizable order; and at the end of the room, near a large window that looked out into a courtyard, there was a beautiful, elaborately carved wooden crucifix. His eyes became fixed on the religious object.

Seth had seen hundreds, maybe thousands of these symbols of the Christian faith, but for the first time in his seventy years, at this moment sitting in Father Juan's office, on the grounds of St. Mary's Catholic Church, the old sheriff was stunned into silence.

"It's beautiful, isn't it?" Father Juan said turning obliquely in his chair to look at the Savior on the Cross. "It was a gift from my father when I was ordained. It was carved in my native country of El Salvador. It never fails to capture the attention of those who see it. I've had a few souls cry in its presence."

Father Juan returned squarely to his guest and again leaned slightly forward. He waited for a moment, but then he asked, "You're not a Catholic, are you, Seth?"

The question brought the man on the couch back from where he drifted. He shifted his eyes toward the priest and cleared his throat softly and offered a one word reply, "No."

"Deborah told me you were not specific about the purpose of your visit, so what is it a small parish priest can offer you?"

Seth didn't respond immediately but looked first into the father's eyes, and then at his own hands folded in a tight knot in his lap.

Abruptly, Father Juan stood up and rolled his chair back to the wall. "Come with me, Seth. I think it might be easier to talk if we take a walk together." The priest extended his hand as an invitation and motioned toward the office door. The sheriff obediently stood and followed Father Juan out the door and towards the front entrance.

"Deborah, Seth and I are going to take a walk around the grounds for a bit. You're now in charge of all emergencies until we get back," the priest smiled at his secretary. They both knew that this little joke was a code for please see that I'm not disturbed.

"Okay, Father. Will do my best," the secretary said and nodded towards the two men as they walked out into a bright day.

First the pair climbed a steep hill that led away from the rectory, and then came to a split in the sidewalk that veered to the right which ended in a parking lot, and to the left that led to the church sitting apart on the highest part of the grounds. Father Juan took the path to the left with Seth at his side. Neither man had yet spoken.

Father Juan, without looking at his companion, said, "I think I know the best place to have our discussion."

The two men entered the church, and the father led Seth Ironwood down the center aisle to about the mid-point in the rows of wooden pews arrayed along both sides. Father Juan, without ceremony, genuflected slightly towards the altar, crossed himself and entered a pew-row on the right and sat down. Seth followed without the religious gestures and sat down next to the priest. Both sat quietly and stared at the Tabernacle with the large crucifix with its sadly humbled figure of Jesus dominating above.

Finally the priest, with his gaze still fixed on the front of the church, said, "Do you ever pray, Seth?"

After a moment in the quiet and still church Seth answered, "No, Father, I don't."

"Would you be willing to tell me why?"

Seth cleared his throat quietly before he answered.

"I guess it's because I'm not very good at it. I haven't prayed since I was a kid. And, I guess I wouldn't know what to say to God if I did. I've been away from Him for most of my life."

"Is that part of the problem you're having in beginning our conversation now?"

Seth nodded his head slightly, almost unseen, in agreement. "Yes, Father, I think that's it. You see, I've spent so many years listening to lies, I mean suspects who are saying whatever they think it will take to get them out of a jam, that I'm not sure anyone can really tell the truth: even myself." Seth turned slightly toward the priest. Father Juan responded in kind, and the two met each other's gaze.

"What I mean to say is that I'm not sure I can tell God the truth. And I don't want to say anything if it's not that. I've made enough mistakes in my life already."

Seth turned back and looked toward the Cross. "Father, I need to get something done soon." He leaned his forearms against the pew in front. "And...and I need to get it right." Seth slightly turned toward the priest. "Does that make sense?"

"Seth, when I was a young lad in El Salvador my *tio*; my uncle, was a priest in a little town called Augullares. I really liked my uncle; he was sort of my best friend. I guess that was one of the reasons I became a priest myself. Well, one of the things he always said to me about my prayers to God; he liked to tell me they weren't as much prayers as they were conversations. Well, what he said was that when I prayed I sent a messenger bird to Heaven. He said it was a raven, like the first bird that Noah dispatched from the Ark hoping to find dry land after the great flood. Well Father Toby, that was what everyone called my uncle; believed that if I said that prayer with a sincere and open heart that the black raven would turn white before it reached its destination. He said that the angels would recognize the white bird as it approached and make sure God got the message." Father Juan, as he finished his story, reached down under the pew in front and pulled down the kneeling bench.

"Seth, would you be willing to pray with me now? Be willing to send a raven to God? That might be the best place to start. What do you say?" The father waited for Seth's answer.

Without a word, Seth awkwardly took the position of prayer with his knees on the bench, and he folded his hands and stared down, wondering whether he was doing it right.

Father Juan joined him and began.

Our Father who art in Heaven, Hallowed be Thy name; Thy Kingdom come, Thy will be done, On earth as it is in Heaven. Give us this day our daily bread; And forgive us our trespasses, As we forgive those who trespass against us; And lead us not into temptation, But deliver us from evil.

In the name of the Father, the Son, and the Holy Spirit we pray. Amen.

Father Juan made the sign of the Cross and waited for a moment. He eased himself back to the pew, and the sheriff followed his lead.

"Seth, do you think that raven will be white when it gets to God?"

"Father, I can only say that coming from you, it probably will. Yes, I suppose it will be."

"You know, Seth, it's really not that difficult to talk to God. In fact, once you get started you'll find that He is one of the easiest to talk to. You just have to do like my uncle said. You have to think about sending white ravens to God. You have to be sincere in your heart, just say what is really there no matter what it is. Once you do that, I promise you He will hear you, and He will respond. And whatever is troubling you now, whatever brought you to this church and to me this day will begin to be less of a burden on you."

Seth turned to Father Juan. "Father," he paused momentarily, "Father, do you think someone like me, I mean this old, worn-out sheriff, could join your parish?"

"Seth, that door at the front opens at all times to all people. Yes, even old worn-out sheriffs. All that's required is that you make the choice. God is waiting, and He will welcome you like no other welcome you have ever had."

The two men sat quietly for a few more moments, and then Father Juan stood up and walked out of the pew into the center aisle. They left the church and moved back out into the light of the day. It was very bright. Sheriff Ironwood reacted to the intense light the way he normally did; he reached into his shirt pocket and took out his sunglasses. But then, as he and Father Juan walked in silence, he hesitated and thought better of the dark filters. He deliberately folded the earpieces back against the lenses and returned the military-style glasses to their storage.

As the two neared the entrance to the office, Seth stopped. Father Juan took a step but then, too, turned to face the sheriff.

"Seth, what is it?"

"Father, can you tell me what to do?"

"You mean about joining this parish?"

"I do. I need…I mean I must do this. I've waited too long. But, Father, there is something else. There's something I'm not sure I can even explain. It's just a feeling; it comes out of nowhere, at any time. It even wakes me with a start from my sleep."

Seth paused and looked down at his boots. "It started just after my wife died. Sometimes I even wonder about my sanity."

Again Seth hesitated. "I don't know...this is just not the time...I mean...."

Father Juan turned back toward the office and took a step. "Seth, let's take it one step at a time. And that first step is to bring you into the parish. Come with me, we'll take a look at the path."

The two men fell into lock-step, but then the father stopped and put his hand on Seth's forearm and stopped him.

"Seth, I want you to know that you've made two of us very happy today," he said with a smile that was broad and warm.

Seth appeared puzzled, "Two, Father?"

"Yes, the one you sent the white raven to back in the church and now to me."

As they walked through the door into the office, Debbie greeted the two with a grin.

"Deborah," Father Juan said, "it appears we're going to get a bit of earthly law enforcement in our pews."

Debbie, unlike her usual demeanor didn't smile, but turned to the sheriff.

"Sheriff Ironwood, there was a call for you about ten minutes ago. It was one of your deputies. She just said that as soon as you get back to come quickly to the department. *Just come quick* is all she said."

The sheriff turned, but quickly turned back toward Father Juan and extended his hand.

"I better see to this, but I'll be back soon, Father. Thanks." He turned briefly toward Debbie and nodded his farewell and mouthed a thank-you to the parish secretary.

As he reached the door, the sheriff again turned. "Soon, Father, soon."

Father Juan walked to the window and watched the tall man with the badge get into his patrol car and abruptly leave the parking lot of St. Mary's.

"Deborah, call the sheriff's office this afternoon and see if you can set up an appointment for me with Sheriff Ironwood. I want to talk to him in his world. There's something he wants me to know that I don't think he can tell me here." Father Juan continued to stare out the window.

"Oh, and Debbie, gather some materials on the process for conversion that I can give Seth. I want to bring this man into our parish as soon as we can. It is hard to put my finger on it exactly, but I can't help but think there's more to the sheriff than we know."

"Father?"

Father Juan did not answer Deborah's inquiry and started towards his office, but then paused and turned again to face his secretary.

"We sent a white raven when we were in the church; the sheriff and I," he said almost sternly. "I have a suspicion that I might get an answer to that message soon enough."

The father smiled briefly a smile that conveyed something other than cheer as he disappeared through his office door.

†

First Blood

Memories in the blood

CARLTON DILLARD WINSTON III, was overjoyed as he hastily tore the dull tan coverings from the cardboard box. He couldn't wait to see and put his hands on the contents. He knew what was inside the carefully wrapped package because the shipping label read *Re_N_Actor's Central Depot & Stores*, Monroe, Michigan. Carlton had, with increasing impatience, waited almost three weeks for this prize; and he tore through the paper and tape as if a starving man tearing into a feast, scattering package remnants in chat-sized pieces haphazardly all over the dining room's hardwood floor.

He was possessed. He had been for months, and the uniform that he now lifted from the crumpled wrappings would finally allow him live out that possession. The blue fabric and the shiny buttons and ribbons glistened as he briefly held the upper part of the uniform in front of his body. He couldn't wait. Carlton was a tall, lanky man in his mid-forties; but now he rushed to the bedroom like a kid that had finally received a long awaited toy from mail order. He tossed the pants, still enshrouded in paper, onto the bed but quickly spun around and pinned the neatly cut jacket up to his torso. He then stared in amazement at the image that looked back from the oversized mirror that dominated the wall over the chest.

No longer was he Carlton Winston. No, Carlton Winston was nowhere to be seen in this reflection. He was a man from many years ago. He was a character from a scene that had been all but forgotten by most. He was a heroic figure; he was proud and gallant. The man that stared back was as far from Carlton as Carlton wished to be from his everyday reality and his irrelevant life in Lawrence, Kansas.

Hurriedly he completed the metamorphosis. He pulled up the blue trousers with the gold stripes that distinguished each leg and buckled the belt. And then he collapsed onto the bench at the foot of the bed and struggled to pull on the stiff boots: wonderfully black and elegant riding boots that marked, more than anything else about the uniform, the mounted soldier; the troopers of the Seventh Cavalry of the United States Army. Carlton completed the dressing as he tied the yellow bandana around his neck and donned the officer's hat with the crossed sabers radiating grandly over the front of the brim.

Kicking packing material out of his way, he stepped back from the mirror and stood erect, at a stance of attention that only the military man can master. Carlton stood frozen in place for over a minute attempting to digest the ghost that stood rigidly before him. He didn't want to move but finally, unable to restrain his emotion, he did. The man, who was now fully reincarnated, briskly saluted his image.

"Major Joel H. Elliott, East Column, commanding, U.S. 7th Cavalry, reporting as ordered, General." As much as he resisted the urge, Carlton broke into a broad grin, but immediately he suppressed that most insubordinate look.

"Sorry sir, I forgot myself for a moment. I anxiously await your orders, General Custer. I will follow you into the depths of the fiery furnace if that be your desire, sir. Yes, into the breach of hell." Again, Major Elliott saluted his image. This time he turned to the side to admire the profile and savor the moment. He hadn't felt this good in years.

Carlton was about to go to the closet and retrieve his Colt revolver to complete his transformation when the doorbell rang. The chime partially invaded the mood, but he pushed back at the invasion and decided not to answer it.

The doorbell rang again; persistently this time, it sounded three times in rapid succession.

"Okay, okay, hold on," Carlton muttered to himself. He self-consciously tossed the cavalry hat onto the bed and pulled off the bandana from around his neck before leaving the bedroom and moving into the long hall that divided the house north from south.

Peeping through the privacy-hole in the front door, he saw a Fed Ex delivery truck parked out front and the delivery man making his way back to it. Carlton let it drive away before he opened the door. Then he caught sight of the large red and white envelope leaning against the porch railing.

There was no indication on the stiff packet as to where it was from or who had sent it. It simply bore Carlton's name and address; but then, the man wedged between the nineteenth and twenty-first centuries, noticed that a large label marked *confidential* was stickered just below his name. He noticed something else. There appeared to be a red smudge lightly overlaying his address. It began just to the right of his last name and trailed off to the lower right of the envelope until it faded and finally disappeared altogether. Carlton thought it curious but quickly forgot the stain as he walked back to the bedroom; He pulled the tab that opened the mailing, and entered the room. As he opened the envelope and peered inside he could see what looked like a letter, and under it was a neatly folded piece of tissue paper.

Carlton delayed his curiosity about the contents long enough to re-dress; to transform like some theatrical superman in a phone booth, to the hero Major Elliott. First he retied the bandana, and then positioned the hat at a slight cocked angle to suggest a jaunty swagger. At last he retrieved the pistol from the closet and secured it in its holster and fastened the leather flap.

Once again he took a step back and admired the officer in the mirror; he offered another salute from a rigid posture of attention. With these formalities completed the soldier sat down on the bed, retrieving and placing the Colt next to him, after cocking the pistol's hammer and releasing it several times.

Then Carlton turned his attention to the strange envelope, withdrawing the contents slowly. First he placed the paper, neatly folded and sealed with a wax-tab, next to the pistol; and then gingerly grasped the tissue paper. As he removed it, he noticed again the same red color smudged on one corner. He laid the tissue next to the folded paper which he assumed had writing on the inside.

Carlton hesitated, why he wasn't sure. For a long moment he just stared at the two items. Again he picked up the envelope; he searched for a clue as to who might have sent them. But he did no better this time with that, so he selected first the folded paper, then he laid it back down and took the tissue in his hand. It was the same kind of tissue that he had seen often in his wife's packages from the department stores. It was thin but strong, elegant but sturdy. He fingered the wrappings gently. The whole piece was light. Whatever was inside didn't have any heft at all.

Finally, Carlton put his index finger inside the fold and pushed it open. After undoing the several folds in the paper he came to its contents. Now he could see why there had been no weight to the package. Inside the tissue was only a feather. It was a wide and long feather with beautifully contrasted colors ranging from a deep, robust brown which transitioned into pure black and finally at its point a brilliant and pristine white. Clean except for the very tip. The tip was caked with an incongruent and dried red substance. It was the same color as the smudges Carlton had noted on the package. He lightly touched the tip, and a few flakes of the red cake broke free and sprinkled onto his cavalry trousers. He quickly brushed them onto the floor. He stared at the beautiful feather; must be an eagle's feather he thought.

Then it dawned on Carlton what this was about. It made sense. This had to be from one of the other reenactors: one of his comrades-in-arms; one of those other soldiers who would again charge the Cheyenne on the Washita River in just a few weeks' time. He speculated for a moment on which one it might have been who sent this package. He picked up the folded paper and turned it over twice to check for an inscription; there was none. Strangely, he wanted to linger over the game; playing it for a moment more before getting to its message.

He didn't know most of the others who would wear the uniforms of Custer's Seventh Cavalry and would soon ride the slopes of the Washita River and into the middle of Black Kettle's sleeping lodges. He had only met most of them once at their meeting in Oklahoma City; where the volunteers gathered to plan the event. He had met none of the Indians who had been recruited to portray the Cheyenne and Arapaho.

Carlton tore open the paper and stared at the note. A cold sweat broke out on his forehead as he quickly absorbed the few lines of writing. He read it over again and paused for almost a minute seeking to understand the message. His mind raced between twin poles of joke and threat. As he thought it out, he alternated a slight laugh and feeble smile with a look that belied the brave cavalry officer of old whose uniform he now wore. A joke, this was a joke. Major Elliot stared back at Carlton Winston from the mirror and helped him come to this conclusion.

Carlton no longer felt like pretending. His stomach was queasy so he quickly undressed, neatly folding the uniform and placing each piece carefully on the end of the bed. He returned the revolver to the high shelf in the closet, covering the weapon with his cavalry hat. He thought about calling his wife but thought better of it. There would be no way she could understand the message. She wasn't in to the historical fascinations and fantasy as he. He decided to let that wait until she returned from her business trip in a week.

He took a beer from the fridge and sat down on the couch. The cold lager settled his stomach and his nerves. He opened his smartphone directory and dialed the number under Joseph Humboldt's name.

"Hello," the voice responded.

✝

Drunken Soldier

Watch my back

SAMUEL JOHNSON was drunk. He had been for months, but tonight he was in the fog more than most. He was alone in the house and it was a good thing. The way he was swinging the four-foot polished steel saber made it perilous for anyone close at hand. Sam wasn't sure where his wife and the boys had gone. He figured to a movie; that's where they normally went when he was in this condition. He never hurt them, but he scared the hell out of his family, and they took to being gone a lot lately.

Sam didn't really care anymore. He liked having the house to himself anyway; so he could pretend. Pretending was his thing, he was good at it. He was better at making believe than he was at living reality. The consequence was that Sam Johnson's life was unraveling; and as it did, he sought shelter more than ever in another life, one he could control.

He mixed another gin and tonic, walked to the back of the

house and peered into the yard through the glass in the back door. Katy's little yapper, as Sam called him, was doing just that at the end of his tie. He hated that little shit dog. He wished he had the courage to take his long-sword and walk up to that nothing of a mutt and slit him open from ears to tail. But instead he took another sip from the glass and savored the soft sting of the liquid as he walked by the hall mirror and paused for another evaluation of his dress and stature. His captain's bars made him feel just fine. He sipped at his drink.

"Well, aren't you a fine looking officer, Capt. Louis M. Hamilton?" Sam rotated to take another look at the profile. "Yes sir. You're the one to command the Left Wing; that you are." He extended his arm with the sword showing the way of the charge down the hall. The tip of the blade struck a small vase on the shelf; it crashed to the floor and shattered with an explosion of tiny pieces.

"Shit!" Sam yelled as he stepped back from the mess of shards and bits of artificial flowers across the hallway. He sat his glass down on the phone stand and his sword on the kitchen counter as he made his way for the broom on the back porch. Just then he saw the car lights pull up the driveway.

"Shit, shit, shit!" he muttered. "Now ain't this just perfect." He ran for the broom and then back to the point of disaster and began to sweep the pile of debris up into a small mound.

"Wow! What happened here?" Katy said as she came around the corner into the hallway. "Here, let me help you, honey."

"Dammit, I can do this. It was a fucking accident. I don't

know why you have to have all of this knick-knack shit stuff all over the house anyway. You can't walk through here without knocking something over. Get back! You're walking in the broken glass."

Katy wanted to say it would be fine if Sam could walk straight, but she held her tongue. The woman was about done with arguing with her husband. In fact, as she watched him clumsily attempt to clean up the mess, she suddenly realized she was done with Sam altogether. She was glad she had left the boys at her mother's. They could stay there until she sorted things out.

"Oh, there's a Fed Ex envelope for you on the kitchen table. It was on the front porch. Your name is on the address label," Katy said as she navigated her way around Sam and into the bedroom.

"Who's it from?"

"I didn't see a sender's name. Don't know."

Katy sat down on the bed and stared at the closet. The door was open, and she could see her clothes neatly arranged along two rows of the big walk-in space. She could see also the suitcases tucked in the corner. She looked at both in turn and mentally calculated how many of her clothes she could take in one trip. She heard the crash of glass falling to the bottom of the metal trash can, and she reflexively tensed her body.

"Who did you say it was from?" Sam asked again in a louder voice.

Katy sighed out loud. "I said, there wasn't a return address," she deliberately pronounced each word so as to penetrate Sam's fog.

"I'll just take the stuff I need for work," Katy muttered to herself.

Sam came into the bedroom holding the envelope and sat his glass on the dresser before sitting down on the bed next to his wife.

"Wonder what the hell this is," he said as he pulled the tab to open the mysterious mailing.

"Sam, we have to talk about something," Katy ignored the question. "Things are just not...."

"Hey! Hold on a minute. Look at this." Sam withdrew the folded paper sealed on one end with red wax and the larger wrapping of tissue paper held closed by a small piece of sticky tape. "What the hell do you suppose this is?" Sam, not too gently, tore at the thin paper and extracted the feather. Katy waited for the opportunity to interrupt, but she finally concluded that she wasn't going to get her chance, so she fell silent and watched her husband.

"It's a damn eagle feather I think. And look at this stuff on the tip. Son-of-a-bitch! It looks like dried blood." Sam rubbed his thumb and forefinger together and flaked some of the red powder onto the bed covers. Katy instinctively brushed them off.

"Here, read this for me. My vision is a bit blurred," Sam said as he popped the note apart and handed it to Katy.

"Sam, please. I need...."

"Dammit, Katy, just read it first. Okay?"

With a slight sigh, Sam's wife took the paper and opened it fully. She read:

One hundred thirty-three years ago General Custer and you led the left flank of the Seventh Calvary through the icy waters of the Washita River. There you savagely attacked the village of my spiritual ancestor, Black Kettle, Chief of the

Cheyenne. You murdered on that bitterly cold, gray morning without regard to sex or age. Most of your people have forgotten this injustice, but I have not. With this letter comes to you an eagle feather stained with the blood of my people; the blood of Black Kettle. It is my blood, and now I will come for yours. Watch for me, it will be soon.

The Spirit of Blood Feather, a son of the Cheyenne

Both husband and wife sat motionless, not speaking. Katy read the text over to herself slowly. On its face, the contents made no sense to her. Katy hadn't paid much attention to her husband's obsession with the history of the cavalry, or his particular passion for the general that Sam was always talking about. She knew his name was Custer, but that was about all she knew. Katy simply dismissed it as a grown-up man's wish to return to his boyhood fantasies.

"It's a joke, a joke, right, Sam?"

Samuel Johnson heard several words from the message, but he hadn't been able to absorb the entire intent. As he thought about *It is my blood,* he said, "Read it again, Katy. Slowly."

Katy didn't argue, and did as Sam asked. She noticed that his usually casual attention had taken on a more determined mood.

She finished for the second time and again asked, "A joke from one of your buddies; right?"

"Yeah," Sam answered. "Must be a joke."

Katy waited for a moment. "Sam, I'm going to...."

Sam appeared not to hear his wife and got up off the bed. He was holding the stained feather in his left hand as he picked up his near-empty glass and walked out of the room without a word. Katy sat still and listened. All she heard was her husband mixing another drink in the kitchen. She stood up and went into the closet and retrieved the large suitcase. She threw it on the bed and opened the lid.

✝

IRONWOOD

Chasing a spirit

SHERIFF SETH IRONWOOD slowly leaned back in his swivel chair and interlocked his long bony fingers behind his head. He stared first for a moment at the ceiling and then at the red face that looked at him, without expression, from across the desk. The sheriff was making an effort to suppress a chuckle as he spoke.

"Now let me get this straight, son. You say you've murdered two men and you're set to make it three if I don't arrest you; have I got that right?"

"Yes," was the stoic reply.

"Okay." Ironwood again spun around in his chair and scooted toward the door of his office. He leaned out the door, without leaving his seat, and shouted, his shout echoing down the long hallway.

"Deputy Stark, if you're in the building I need you to come in here, now if you don't mind." The sheriff waited for a response.

"Stark!"

"Yeah, Sheriff, I hear you. Be there in a sec."

Undersheriff Raaven Stark quickly tied back her long hair and grabbed her note pad from the upper drawer of her desk as she started for the sheriff's office. The deputy had seen the Indian man go into Ironwood's office and she suspected she might be needed to interpret. She didn't think he looked Cheyenne though, but she wasn't sure. She figured he was more of mixed-blood.

"Yes, Sheriff," she said as she came into the office and glanced first at the person who sat rigid in front of the sheriff's desk and then at the sheriff.

"Pull up a chair, Deputy, this may take a while. This lad here, believe it or not, claims to be a serial killer. Hardly looks like the type to me." The sheriff turned his head slightly so that the confessor couldn't see him raise his eyebrow as he looked at Deputy Stark.

"I want you to take down all the details of this extraordinary admission," the sheriff said as he rose and walked to his office door. He quietly pushed it shut and returned to his desk.

The old lawman looked for a long moment at the man who sat like a stone figure in front of him. Finally he said, "I want to make sure...tell me your name again, son."

The man hesitated, as if he didn't understand the question, but finally responded.

"My Indian name is Wolf That Follows."

"What's your Christian name?"

Again the man hesitated, finally he said, "I don't have one."

"Well I suppose we will have to stop right there until we can come up with one. "

The would-be confessor for a while remained fixed in place and expressionless.

"It's Simon, Simon Peter Straw."

"That's better. And where do you hail from, Mr. Straw?"

"What?"

"Where do you live, son?"

"South Dakota, Pine Ridge. Or, I did until recently."

"The reservation?"

"Just outside."

"Okay. You see, Mr. Straw; I want to make absolutely sure you understand what you're doing. Confessing to a murder is bad enough, but confessing to several murders and the intent to do others is a bit over the top so to speak; especially around here in Custer County. So if you need to think about this for a moment that will be quite understandable." The sheriff leaned back in his chair and waited for a reply.

The man said nothing, and likewise waited. The silence was the loudest noise in the room so again the sheriff let his seat find center and asked another question.

"Do you want a lawyer present? It is your right along with the right to remain silent, and the right not to incriminate yourself. What I'm telling you, Mr. Straw, is that whatever you say to me now, in front of my deputy, can and most likely will be used against you in a court of law. Do you recognize and acknowledge these rights, son?"

This time there was no hesitation. "I do, Sheriff," he said as he glanced at Deputy Stark who was now sitting with a pad on her lap and a pen in her hand taking notes.

"All right then, if it be your desire, let's hear it," the sheriff nodded toward the deputy.

"Be sure and get as much detail as you can, Deputy. I've got a feeling this is going to take quite a bit of investigation."

As the man began his tale, Sheriff Ironwood suddenly sensed that this might not be an ill-conceived joke. As he heard the beginning of the story, he felt as if he was hearing it from Wolf That Follows, the Indian; and that Simon Peter Straw didn't exist: at least not the one sitting in the chair in front of his well-worn desk.

"The first man I killed was Major Joel H. Elliott. I killed him with my knife. I pierced his heart with the blade. I took his scalp, and then I removed his eyes so he could not see his comrades in the afterlife." At this admission, the man reached into his shirt pocket and took out a piece of folded paper that, when he put it on the desk in front of the sheriff, appeared to be slightly stained.

"And, what is that, Mr. Straw?"

"Proof of what I say. It is some of Elliott's hair; a part of his scalp that I took."

Sheriff Ironwood nodded toward Raaven Stark. "Better get an evidence bag for this," he said without touching the folded paper.

"Well, that is quite an admission, I grant you that. Would you care to explain why you killed this...this Major Elliott?"

Simon Peter sat rigid as if he wasn't going to answer.

"Mr. Straw, I really think...."

"I did it to make justice for my people," he interrupted; "to make justice for the wrongs done to my spiritual father, Black Kettle. That's why I killed the two men, and will kill the third if you do not arrest me now."

"Okay, I understand that part; the part about you not

wanting to continue with the murders. What is not the least bit clear is all the rest. So now, what I've got so far," looking at Raaven, "and, what I hope you have as well, Deputy, is that you, Mr. Straw murdered, with a knife a Major Elliott in revenge for what Major Elliott did to your spiritual father? Is that it?"

"It was not revenge; it was justice."

The sheriff stared for a moment at young man, "Okay, I'll let that go for now. You killed the man for some reason you call just. Okay, now where did this killing take place?...near Pine Ridge?"

"No, I killed them both near here on the Washita River; close to where the Cheyenne lodges once stood."

"You're speaking of the National Washita Battleground site, right? Over near Cheyenne?"

"Yes, that is the place."

"All right, Mr. Straw. We have the person, we have the place, we have the method, we have the motive, I think. Now, when did you do this killing?"

"The day of the battle."

"Battle? What battle would that be?" Ironwood again glanced at his deputy hoping to get some clarification. He only got a shrug of the shoulders in return.

"Mr. Straw, I'm not familiar with any recent battles having occurred around...," the sheriff hesitated. "Wait! Wait just a minute. You wouldn't be talking about that reenactment thing they did last month would you? The reenactment of that historical battle thing between Custer's Seventh Cavalry and the Cheyenne...of course you are. Chief Black Kettle, right? The Peace Chief, right? The one Custer's men killed way back then. That's it isn't it?"

"Yes."

Sheriff Ironwood looked up at the ceiling for a long moment and then he returned his gaze, more intense this time, to Simon Straw.

"Mr. Straw, you are going to have to pardon me, but I'm going to be blunt with you. You see, I think you might be off your nut as they say. That was a reenactment. You didn't kill those men. You played like you killed them. It was no more than a show, son. Are you on some kind of medication, or drugs, or what?"

The sheriff got up from his chair and circled his desk. As he did he dragged his chair with him and sat down directly facing Simon Straw.

"Okay. What is this about? You are dangerously close to getting yourself in a really sticky mess with this wild tale of yours. Do I make myself clear?"

"I killed their spirit."

"You did what?"

"I killed their spirit, Sheriff." Simon looked directly at the sheriff as he spoke the second time. "I killed those murderers. Their spirits are dead...lost forever."

"I see," the sheriff said as he stood up and returned his chair back behind his desk. He remained quiet for a long minute as he studied the face of Simon Straw. He cut his eyes towards his deputy for a second before he turned back to the young man.

"You want to tell me, Mr. Straw, what this is really about?" Sheriff Ironwood waited.

Simon Peter Straw lowered his eyes to the floor, but didn't answer the sheriff's question.

"Son, I don't know what you are up to with this fantasy

tale; but, if you persist, I'm going to find out, and, I suspect you are going to regret what you are doing. So, one last time, what is this about?"

The sheriff again looked in the direction of Deputy Stark. She met his eyes and slightly shook her head indicating to the sheriff that she couldn't offer any help with the young man's story.

Finally the sheriff stood up and walked to the front of his desk and sat down on the corner as he pushed a stack of papers out of the way. He continued to look at Simon Peter for a long moment.

"Okay, Mr. Straw. I guess you can have it your way…for now." The sheriff faced his deputy. "Deputy, would you take Mr. Straw to booking, and find him some accommodations until we sort this out."

Simon Peter finally raised his head and let his eyes meet that of the sheriff. Ironwood waited for a second, but the man didn't say anything.

"Okay, Deputy, that's it. Escort our prisoner to booking, and let's get to other business…Oh! Wait a sec. Simon, I have one more question. You have any relatives around here that you would like to call? Mother, brother, uncle, anybody?"

The sheriff waited. Finally Simon Peter simply said, "No."

"All right then…Deputy Stark, Mr. Straw is in your care."

✝

THE SECOND COMING

Next to the last stand

THE TALL LANKY MAN bounded energetically up on the stage and peered for an extended moment at the large crowd gathered in audience for his performance. Then, partly to dispel the minor nervousness he felt in his gut; the man draped in a magnificent uniform of a cavalry officer from a time distant with a lengthy flowing red scarf tied nonchalantly around his neck, began to take long graceful strides along the front of the stage. As he did, he eagerly absorbed the rumble of the applause: applause that never ceased to fill his soul and freed him to complete the metamorphosis from communal citizen to *The General*.

While the wave of excitement flowed up from those who occupied the well-ordered rows of chairs, *The General*, George Armstrong Custer, crisply withdrew his saber; and, standing as straight and rigid as his six-foot, four-inch frame could muster; he saluted the crowd with the formality and flamboyance of the nineteenth-century cavalry officer that he now was. The roar that confirmed the transition produced waves of thunder through the hall, sending shivers of exhilaration coursing through the body of the well-appointed reenactor. He was reborn, alive to his true nature, to his true spirit. To Alex Austenne there was no greater rush; no greater honor than this long-studied portrayal.

The elegant cavalry officer waited for the crowd to calm, gracefully returning his sword to its sheath with a restrained display of military showmanship. *The General* again began to stride slowly along the stage as he fixed his gaze, first on one, and then another of his admirers. He loved the look they returned. They, too, lived for the fantasy; transported, like Alex, to another time and place.

Then, with a bit of drama in his hesitation, he turned squarely to the rows of seated anticipation and deliberately began his monologue.

You ask me, what of the Red Man, he said and then paused. Again he stared into the eyes of a well-chosen few, affecting a bond between spirits pursuing the same cause. He glanced briefly at his shiny boot tops, hesitating briefly, seeking the proper rhythm for the reading to come. Alex had long ago memorized every word taken from the writings of the man he admired beyond all those in history. Suddenly he felt all was just as it should be. Repressing a smile of excitement, *The General* continued...

What will become of the Red Man? You say...Here then is your answer.

Alex raised his eyes slowly, and as he did, he visualized the written word of his champion. He had spoken these words so many times that the man, now dressed as the most famous Indian fighter, couldn't prevent himself from believing that what he spoke on this stage, he had written as well.

*When we first beheld the Red Man...*he projected over the crowd in a soft voice that forced many in the hall to reflexively shift slightly forward in their seats...*we beheld him in his home of peace and plenty, the home of nature. Sorrows furrowed lines were not weakened by being forced to sleep in dreary caves and deep morasses, fireless, comfortless and coverless, through fear of the hunter's deadly rifle. His heart did not quake with terror at every gust of wind that sighed through the trees, but on the contrary, they were the favored sons of nature, and she like a doting mother, had bestowed all her gifts on them. They stood in the native strength and beauty, stamped with the proud majesty of free-born men, whose souls never knew fear, or whose eyes never quelled beneath the fierce glance of men. But what are they now, those monarchs of the West? They are like withered leaves of their own native forest, scattered in every direction by the fury of the tempest. The Red Man is alone in his misery...*

The General stood erect and rigid as he waited for the effects of the ancient rhetoric to settle over the crowd like a soft mist. As he moved his eyes from one to another without turning his head, he noticed a man in a middle row slowly rise from his seat. Alex was used to this. Many of his admirers often couldn't contain their emotions as they heard the words of their ancient hero. But this one was different; and as he stood tall and conspicuous among all the others, Alex sensed it immediately.

"Murderer!"

"Murderer!" came the shout again from the man standing.

The sudden outburst split the atmosphere in the hall like a bolt of lightning on a summer night.

"You are the murderer of my people!" the man roared again, this time in such a forceful, bass voice that the hall shook in the wake of the vibration.

The effect of the outcry was no less than if the earth had stopped its rotation and time had stopped with it. *The General*, standing alone on the stage, felt as if he had come to a cosmic standstill: a sensation complemented by the stunned silence that now hushed all in the expanse of the hall.

Both men stared at one another. Their eyes locked as if a trance had taken over both souls; had taken command of these two as if no others were present, two warriors alone on the battlefield, preparing for the clash of arms.

Then, as the first shocked reactions came from the audience; at first merely a low-volume pool of murmurs, the young man calmly broke off his gaze and made his way to the exit aisle. What began as a soft rumble finally burst forth into an angry thunder of shouts. The stranger seemed to be unaffected, and calmly left the hall without another word; without even a glance back to the tall man with ancient golden locks and a red scarf standing solitary and stiff on the stage in silence.

The General remained unmoving as he watched the offender depart. He paid heed to the long, braided black hair that hung almost to the waist of the man, and he realized that this must have been the only Indian in the hall.

Suddenly he understood that what he had long feared would happen, had now finally happened. The ancient character he played with such acumen, such realism, such affected enthusiasm, now had stirred in another the feeling that *The General* was again amongst the living: was again to be not only admired and revered, but also scorned and fiercely hated.

Alex, instinctively, bowed slightly to the man as he disappeared through the doors, and vanished into the dark beyond the soft lighting of the auditorium. There continued a low, collective murmur rising like stale smoke from the crowd as Alex sought to recover his place and character.

The General slowly returned to the moment he had lost. In a strong, authoritative voice, he continued the program...

The earth is one vast desert to him. Once it had its charms to lull his spirit to repose, but now the home of his youth, the familiar forests, under whose grateful shade, he and his ancestors stretched their weary limbs after the excitement of the chase, are swept away by the axe of the woodman; the hunting grounds have vanished from his sight and in every object he beholds the hand of desolation. We behold him now on the verge of extinction, standing on his last foothold, clutching his bloodstained rifle, resolved to die amidst the horrors of slaughter, and soon he will be talked of as a noble race who once existed but now have passed away.

The General hesitated once again as he finished the oration. Slowly, with precise formality, he offered a salute to the audience; then he bowed with a melodrama that would fit well the man he portrayed. The spontaneous applause shook the dust from the overhanging light fixtures: the rude outburst of the moments before had already been forgotten by most. Again, it was the ancient hero on the stage that commanded the attention of all in his presence. General George Armstrong Custer lived, and was triumphant.

As he rose from his last bow to his audience and the applause began to fade, Alex glanced toward the front of the hall, at the doors that now stood open to the night beyond. He looked at the darkness just outside the hall, wondered reflexively where the man who had cursed him had gone. The brave cavalry officer thought now how glad he was that his van was parked in the back. The unease was fleeting and disappeared altogether as small gatherings of boisterous fans beseeched *The General* to come and pose for pictures and mingle.

Alex Austenne smiled a sustained and broad smile, keeping his right hand firmly upon the handle of his saber, as he moved graciously and with authority among the crowd. As he spoke to all that inquired of him, the performer once again returned to the man he wanted to be; the man he now was. The spirit of the great soldier now ran through his body like the blood in his veins; it spoke the words that came from his lips. It possessed the man with the bold red scarf tied flamboyantly around his neck as it always had. It was a spirit that could not die; could not be killed.

✝

A WARRIOR'S DREAM

Justice frees,
Revenge entraps

HE DEPUTY came into the sheriff's office abruptly without knocking and pulled up a chair in front of his desk. Ironwood was on the phone, but looked at her with an inquisitive slant of his head as he finished the conversation and hung up.

"Yes, Stark. You have something for me?"

"I do indeed, Sheriff. It's about our young serial killer."

Ironwood leaned back in his swivel chair and intertwined his fingers across his chest.

"Let me guess. It's all a hoax," the sheriff spoke slowly for emphasis. "A big fantasy; a young Indian man's dream, or maybe I should say nightmare. The dream of a warrior from a century ago. Am I right, Stark?"

Raaven slumped in her chair and looked at the sheriff quizzically. "How did you know that?"

"That phone conversation I just had; that was a fellow named Joseph Humboldt. Mr. Humboldt ran the Washita

Battle for the Chamber. He's the guy that put together all the reenactors for the event; both the cavalry soldiers and the Cheyenne Indians for Black Kettle's village. He told me that most of the Indians were locals, but the majority of the Custer troopers traveled from various points in the country...seems that these guys do this as a hobby or something like that. You know, dress up like cavalry, ride horses in a charge; and shoot blanks at Indians. Relive the glory days; that kind of stuff." The sheriff paused, flashing a fake smile and raising his eyebrows for emphasis.

"And?" Raaven played along.

"And, ol' Joe also told me that the two guys that played the cavalry soldiers that our young mass murderer named; that Major Elliot, and the other one...whatever his name was?"

"Hamilton, Captain Hamilton," Raaven filled in the blank.

"Yeah, that's right. Well it seems that both of those men were killed at the original battle, or massacre, or whatever you call it; and more important, the guys that played them in the reenactment were also killed at the reenactment, but with a big difference."

"A big difference?"

"Yeah. You see those two are just as alive as the other ones are dead. So does that have anything to do with what you were going to tell me?"

"Sort of. I mean it does and it doesn't. We got the lab report back on that so-called piece of scalp that Simon Straw gave us."

"Yes. Not human, I'm guessing," the sheriff interrupted.

"No, it's human all right, just not modern human. The lab

guys said in their report that the hair was well over a hundred years old. It was most likely taken back when such things were in fashion. I might add in all fairness, by both sides," the deputy said.

"Well, that's good to know. I never believed that young man's story from the get-go; or maybe I should say, I never wanted to believe it was true. That kid just doesn't fit the profile of a killer. You know?"

"We're on the same page with that, Sheriff."

"But, there is something else I got from Joe Humboldt. Both of those undead cavalry reenactors got a little surprise in the mail. You're going to love this as a Native type. It seems they both received death threats via a mailed package." The sheriff stood up and circled the desk. He sat down on the corner.

"And guess what came with the threat?" The sheriff raised his right eyebrow to encourage the deputy to offer a speculation.

"Let me see. A poisoned arrow?"

"Close, but no cigar. It was a feather; most likely an eagle feather. But here's the kicker...the feather was dipped in what appears to be blood. In fact, the note that accompanied the feather said it was dipped in the blood of the Indian that was going to take revenge on these two guys."

Raaven Stark stood up and did a turn around the office before she said, "Well then, Sheriff, if that is human blood, and maybe the blood of the person who made the threats, then we've got some very strong evidence for at least a willful threat charge."

"Yes, Deputy, we do. Humboldt is overnighting the feathers to me. Give the state lab a call and tell them what we've got and that we will need a quick turn-around on a DNA test. And, see if the young man in our jail will consent to give a blood sample. My guess is that it won't be a match, but we need to make sure."

"And, if it is, Sheriff?"

"Well, let's wait on that. I don't know what it is, but the water is flowing up stream on this thing. Anyway, I want to hold Mr. Straw until we get the results on the blood."

Deputy Stark started for the door, but stopped. "What if he won't consent to the blood sample?"

"Um…I'm not sure. Probably we turn him loose." The sheriff took a step toward the deputy, "Of course, if you could get a bit of hair from our guest…well then, we might be able to do it anyway; you think?"

"Why, Sheriff Ironwood; that sounds a bit underhanded."

The sheriff turned to go back to his desk. "Does, doesn't it? Let your conscience be your guide Deputy; keep me as uninformed as possible. What do they say in Washington…*plausible deniability*?" The sheriff sat down and made a show of shuffling some paperwork without comment.

"Oh, Raaven, there's something else."

Deputy Stark stopped and turned around; she made note of the sheriff calling her by her first name.

"Yes."

"Our young Indian friend has been a bit deceptive with us about relatives here-and-about."

"Really? Surprise, surprise." Raaven took a couple of steps back into the office. "Is his mother somewhere near?"

"His brother…Simon Peter Straw has a brother. That was another little piece of news that Mr. Humboldt laid on me.

And get this...they are identical twins. Humboldt says you can't tell them apart...two sides of the same coin, is how he put it."

Deputy Stark smiled at Sheriff Ironwood. "Well, how about that? I guess the plot begins to thicken; wouldn't you say, Sheriff?"

"I'd say that's a fact. The brother's name is Andrew, I don't have a middle name. See what you can find out about the brother; but Deputy..."

"What, Sheriff?"

"Let's keep that info to ourselves for the time being. Don't mention it to Simon Peter."

"Okay. But, Sheriff, you know that this could pose a problem with our blood-sample, don't you?"

"Problem? How's that?" Sheriff Ironwood again leaned back in his chair.

Deputy Stark sat back down in the chair facing the sheriff. "Well, it's that identical twin thing. It might give us trouble telling one side of that coin from the other, you could say."

"How's that?"

"Well, if those boys were truly born identical, I think the word is monozygotic, it may be hard to tell them apart by their DNA. Like their faces it would be identical."

The sheriff looked sideways at the deputy. "Mono...what?"

"Monozygotic. It means, I think, two embryos come from the same female egg...I think. They're identical because their genetic material is identical."

"You're sure about that?"

"Yes, I'm a twin. Had an identical twin sister, so I know how that stuff works; sort of."

Sheriff Ironwood looked at his deputy for a long moment. "You never told me that, Raaven," he said finally. "Where is she?

"She died, Seth; a long time ago."

The sheriff looked at Raaven and slightly shook his head in recognition.

"I'm sorry, I didn't know."

"That's okay, Seth, you had no reason to know. Like I said, it happened when we were just kids."

"All right," the sheriff shuffled some papers on his desk for a second. "Okay, get the sample if you can, from Simon Peter. We'll let the lab guys work through the science. Okay?"

"Yeah, I'm on it, Sheriff."

"And, Raaven, tell me something."

"What's that?"

"You have any notions as to what our fantasy murderer is up to. I mean, doesn't it seem a bit bizarre to come in here and confess to some murders that never happened. You think this kid is wacko?"

Raaven Stark stood up and walked to the window of the sheriff's office. She stared out into the parking lot for a long moment. "He's not wacko, as you put it, Seth. There's method in his madness, as they say. Simon is smart, and, he certainly doesn't strike me as a trouble-maker. There's something going on with this confession, I just don't have a clue as to what it is. Maybe if we can link him to the feathers and the threatening letters we can get a better handle on it. You think?"

"I hope. I really can't put my finger on it, but this thing is raising the hair on my back for some reason. You know, I've been around this job for a long time, and I have never had one of these cases chill me like this one."

Sheriff Ironwood got out of his chair and joined Deputy Stark at the window. Without turning to face her he said, "You got time for lunch today?"

The deputy hesitated, but then turned around to face the sheriff.

"Yeah, sure. What's up?"

"Nothing. It's just that we haven't visited in a long time outside the office. That's all."

"Okay. Shout at me when you're ready."

"Yeah, I will. We'll make it a late lunch around one o'clock. Okay?"

"That's good with me." Deputy Stark shut the door softly as she left the sheriff's office.

✝

BLUNT TRAUMA

Will it heal?

RAAVEN STARK sat patiently, occasionally sipping from an oversize mug of Colombian dark roast. She stirred it with stick of wood cinnamon and stared at the sheriff's hand as it cradled a cup of java. Ironwood's coffee was the regular house brew without sweetener or cream; simply coffee, the kind long-time lawmen seem to prefer. Raaven could never imagine why; too plain and bitter for her taste.

At last, the sheriff raised his head to look at his deputy. The intensity of his blue eyes always took her a bit by surprise no matter how many times she saw them. They were wells that pulled you to their edges, threatening to suck you over into their black waters deep below.

"You want to know how it feels, do you?" The sheriff took a sip. "I can't imagine why...."

"Sheriff, forget I ever asked. I'm just being nosey; just a woman's curiosity getting the best of her. You really don't have to...."

Sheriff Ironwood ignored his deputy's attempt at politeness, politeness that masked the real emotion of sympathy, and continued.

"Deputy Stark," he said, taking another sip of coffee, "have you ever been stabbed with a screwdriver?" He then paused, as he held the cup in the air, and like magic a pot appeared at the end of a long arm to refill it. "Thanks, Sally," he said without looking up.

"A screwdriver, Sheriff? You said a screwdriver?"

"Yes, a big, blunt-headed straight-slot screwdriver. Stabbed with it?"

Raaven looked at Seth Ironwood askance and let a mischievous smile come to her lips. "Well, no can't say that I have. Got hit pretty hard one time with an axe handle though. That hurt like hell, I can sure tell you."

"About sixteen years ago." The sheriff again paused long enough to take another slurp of his black coffee.

"I had only been on the force for a couple of years, when I was given a warrant to serve on a suspect for burglary. The young fellow, he was about twenty if I remember correctly, worked down at the ProFixx Auto Shop on Copton and 12th. I knew who he was but never had actually spoken with the young man. What I did know of him really wasn't that bad – a few pranks as a teenager, but that was about it. So as I drove to his work location, I double-checked the name on the warrant; just to make sure I was getting the right man. I didn't expect any trouble from this guy.

"As I walked in the front service entrance, the foreman, a fellow I remember went by the name of the Round Man; part Indian I figured, looked up from a magazine he was reading.

"'Round Man,' I called out to him before reaching the counter, and almost laughed as I looked into his face. I couldn't help it; the face fit the name to a tee, just a big, round fat face. In some ways, it resembled one of those happy Buddha statues you see around those gift shops; always smiling, always cheerful on the surface. I knew from the record, however, that this jolly ole boy could be a rounder indeed in a barroom fight. Hoped for none of that this day. Only a simple and routine arrest would suit me.

"Round Man pitched his magazine into a chair that held a collection of the same, exited from behind the counter and reluctantly extended his hand. I gladly took it. The grip was as soft as a kid's teddy bear, but I put some pressure behind mine. The foreman of the shop quickly withdrew his fingers in response to the uncomfortable squeeze.

"'Need an oil change, Sheriff?' he asked while at the same time looking out at the squad car parked across the exit.

"'Not today. Is Travis in the back?'

"Round Man paused as if trying to think of the right thing to say. As sheriff I was used to it so I repeated his question with a bit of a stinger attached for emphasis.

"'Travis back there? I've got a warrant.'

"'What's he done, Sheriff?'

"'I'll be needing to talk to him about that. Is that him out there in that back stall leaning under the bonnet of that Ford pickup?'

"Round Man glanced in that direction and nodded. 'Yes, sir,' he said, 'that's him. Is he in trouble?'

"'Thank you. You might want to keep everybody up in the office until I complete my service.'

" 'Sure, Sheriff, I can do that.'

"Well, I did what I normally do in such cases, I decided to approach the task as squarely as possible. I came up within about five feet of the lad, and he didn't even sense my presence until I called his name.

"'Travis, Travis Koppes?' The boy stood up and I could see his entire body tense. He was an angular type with good muscle tone. And that muscle tone was definitely on display through the back of his tee shirt, which was stained with random lakes of sweat. A second or two passed, but the suspect didn't turn to face me.

"I took one more step closer, and was about to call his name again; in fact, I think I might have said it partially. You see I'm not sure because that's when I got to see his face for the first time, just before I felt the blunt tool penetrate my chest as if it had exploded out of a howitzer. I remember looking down at the blue and yellow alternately striped handle of the tool, I think it said *Craftsman*, but could see none of the shaft."

Sheriff Ironwood stopped his narrative and sipped at the coffee that had become tepid. Again he raised the cup in the air. The magic worked as always; and he took a long sip of the hot liquid.

Finally, Deputy Stark tentatively broke the silence. "Wow! I bet that kind of hurt." The attempt at humor fell flat, and she regretted it as soon as the words were out of her mouth.

"Yeah! Kind of."

"But, Sheriff, not to be interrupting a good tale of the badge, does that have anything to do with what I asked you about losing Mary?"

Seth Ironwood was silent for a long second. "Everything," the sheriff finally answered. As he did, he pulled his slender frame away from the booth-table and leaned back into the soft back padding of the booth. He cocked his head slightly. To Deputy Stark he gave the impression that his mind was reaching out into space, somewhere far from the small diner where the two sat if singularly alone.

The sheriff fixed his gaze on his deputy. "You know, Raaven, what struck me so strange about that day was as I looked down at that shaft firmly implanted in my chest; the doctors said it had barely missed my heart and had punctured my left lung, the thought that rushed over me was not whether *I was going to die*; the thought I had at that moment was whether *I was going to heal if I lived*.

"As I sank to my knees on the floor as if to offer a prayer, and my assailant disappeared, I remember clearly thinking, *would I ever heal? Would I ever be the same?*

"And that question brings us back to your question. If I still remember it rightly, you wanted to know how it feels to lose someone that you love, and lose them in a matter of minutes with no warning; that was the question, right?"

"Yes, Sheriff, that was it; and again I apologize for being so nosey."

"No...no, Deputy, no apologies needed or accepted. These are just the kind of questions that we should share. Life is lonely enough without walling ourselves in behind dense stones. This may satisfy your curiosity, but, Raaven the telling also helps to patch a hole in my soul, if not in my chest.

"You see, Raaven, when Mary collapsed that day into my arms without warning; when she whispered, almost inaudible as she fell, those last three words, *Oh My God,* when I lay her softly onto that cold concrete floor and kneeled helplessly before the power of our Creator, and watched the life of my love leave me as abruptly as flipping a light-switch; the question that flooded my consciousness was that same question that I had had with that ugly screwdriver protruding from my chest. I remember clearly at this moment as I did at that, saying softly to myself, *would I ever heal from such a wound as this?"*

Raaven Stark tried to keep eye contact with the sheriff. It was difficult because the moisture that she saw there was quickly replicated in her own. Finally, not really knowing what to say, she offered, in a rather weak voice, "Well, have you, Seth; have you healed?"

Sheriff Ironwood again leaned forward, rested his elbows on the table and gripped the coffee cup with both hands securely, trying to minimize the shake. He stared into the black liquid for a moment. Then he looked up and met the gaze of the woman across from him.

"Raaven, I can't say the verdict's in yet. I'm beginning to think that some wounds go so deep that there isn't enough time in this life for healing. But, you'll be among the first to know when it comes in."

Seth flashed an unaffected smile at his favorite deputy: a smile that beckoned the end of the story, but then he cleared his throat.

"You know what I miss the most about her, Raaven?" The deputy shook her head and offered a subdued smile.

"It's kind of a selfish thing I know, but what I miss most about Mary is that she was my biggest fan." The sheriff paused and took a sip of coffee.

"She made me feel like I was ten-feet tall. Oh, I'm not saying she didn't criticize me; boy did she ever. There wasn't much that I did that didn't get the once over. But, when I did something right you would have thought I walked on water. And, I'm here to tell you, Raaven, that if you get to walk on water, even just one time, that's enough. You never forget it. That's what I miss the most. Just that chance; just that slight chance that she would say *You're wonderful, Seth.*"

Raaven Stark didn't say anything, because there was nothing to say. She just let the silence be where it was supposed to be.

"Let's order that lunch we came here for; what do you say?" the sheriff said finally. "I'm kind of hungry all of a sudden. How about you?"

"Ravished, I think is the term they use in Dallas, Seth."

"Ravished, it is then. You tell the waitress for us; I don't think Sally will appreciate that term," the tired looking man again smiled. His deputy pushed a well-worn menu across the table and flipped the one in front of her open.

Two full pages of burgers and fries reflected from the list. Raaven couldn't focus on the perfect images through the fog of sadness she felt and the moisture that covered her eyes.

"What looks good, Deputy?"

Raaven stared for a long moment at the perfect pictures of food. "Oh, I don't know, Seth. I'll just have what you have," she said as she closed the menu and stuck it behind the condiment bottles against the dingy wall.

Sheriff Ironwood raised his arm to motion for Sally. The waitress grabbed the coffee pot and headed for the table.

✝

RAAVEN'S WELL

Lost to the underground

SETH STARED unconsciously at his deputy as he pushed the empty plate away and took hold of his coffee cup. When Raaven Stark finally noticed his blank look in her direction, she returned his gaze.

"Oh! Excuse me, Stark, I'm kind of in a fog. Not sure why, just a bit adrift."

"We all have those days, Sheriff; me more than most. Maybe it's a symptom of too much to do and too little time to do it; you think?"

"Yeah, I definitely think. But you know, I'm also thinking that I have been staring at you for a reason. It's a question that I have wanted to ask you for a long time, but just never could find the right time. Maybe this is the right time. You know? Since I told you my dark secret."

"Okay, what would that question be?" Raaven leaned back against the back of the booth.

"Well, it's kind of personal."

"Yeah. That's okay. The question I asked you was kind of personal too," Raaven smiled a curious, inquisitive smile. "What? What's the question, Seth?"

"Well, I've been wondering how you got your name," the sheriff paused and again glanced up at the dirty light fixture above his desk.

"My name?"

"Yeah, Raaven. That's a very unusual name...no? I mean, it's a bird; a big, black bird, right?"

The deputy decided not to answer, but wait and see where the sheriff was going with this.

"Don't get me wrong, I understand that Indians have a long tradition of naming children after animals and other things in nature. I understand that. But, you see, I don't see the connection between you and a big, black bird. After all, you're a very light blond; I mean a natural blond. You are, aren't you?" The sheriff self-consciously cleared his throat. Raaven could see he was having doubts about his inquiry, so she tactfully interrupted.

"Yes. A natural blond, you might say. Not born that way, but natural nevertheless."

"Okay, now you're really confusing me."

Raaven again offered the sheriff a smile. "It is one of those spiritual Indian tales that the *wasichus* don't usually take to, but here's how it happened." Raaven paused. Before she could begin, the waitress stopped at the table, and, without a word, held up the coffee pot. The sheriff just nodded and pushed his cup toward her.

"When me and my sister were born we both were born with a full head of coal black hair," Raaven began after the waitress departed. "My mother said it was so long and luxurious that she could have braided it in my first hours. In fact, she said she couldn't stop brushing our hair with her hands; it was so soft and silky. So, for her, it just seemed natural that this first defining characteristic should also be a name. That's what she did. She told my father to tell the nurse to name me Raven; to name me after the bird with such black and shiny feathers. But somehow when they put that name on my birth certificate it got an extra "a" put into the name. No one caught it until later, much later. By then my mother decided she liked the unusual spelling and just accepted it."

The sheriff interrupted, "So you were born with black hair, not blond?"

"That's right."

"So; how…?"

"Well, that's the mystical part of this story. When I was six years old, me and my sister were playing outside at my grandfather's house with our dolls. We had a bunch of little Kachina-style Indian dolls. I had mine all lined up on the edge of my grandfather's well where he drew his water. I was playing like my friends were dancing the sacred dances all around the edge of the well. Then as careless little girls sometimes do, I accidentally knocked one of my favorite warrior dolls off of the ledge, and it fell into the deep well below. All I remember was that I instinctively reached out to try and catch the doll." Raaven paused.

The sheriff leaned forward in his chair, "I bet that really made you sad, uh?"

"I don't know. I don't remember much. You see, Seth, as I reached to try and catch the doll, I bumped my sister, her name was Maven, and she lost her balance."

"You mean…."

"Yeah, she fell into the well along with the doll. I had all those dolls lined up around the well, when my grandmother came to check on us. I was scared, too scared to tell her, but she knew something was terribly wrong; she frantically looked about for my sister. When she realized what had happened she quickly called my uncles who lived in the next house over, and they desperately tried to get down the well. But it was too late."

"Raaven, I'm sorry I asked you this. I didn't mean..."

"Seth, it's all right. It happened a very long time ago, and I was just a little girl. A little girl that really couldn't understand what had happened. I guess, rationally, I do now, but it's like what you said to me. Some wounds really never heal; you just learn to ignore them for the most part."

"Yeah, you're right. Boy! What a lunch?" Seth said in a soft voice.

"You can say that again. But you asked me how I got my blond hair, and that's really the strange part of this story. You see, within a few weeks of that tragedy, my hair began to change its color. At first, it turned into kind of amber. Then over the next year it changed into the color that it is now: almost a blond-white."

"Wow! Why do you think it did that?"

"Well, nobody could tell us. My mom took me to the doctor, but he couldn't figure it out. My uncle was kind of a medicine man for our family: you know the kind that always had a natural cure for what ailed us. He was convinced that when my twin sister fell into that deep well, she took with her a part of my original spirit to the water down below. And when they were not able to save her, that spirit was lost in the underground with her. He said that spirit was still lost down there somewhere, probably still playing with the *Kachina*. He used to enjoy telling me that someday that spirit would find its way back to me. He said that when it did, my hair would go back to its original color. I don't know about that, but that's how I got my name and how I got my blond hair."

The sheriff just stared at Raaven for a moment. He smiled slightly. "Deputy, I am continually amazed at you. I am one lucky sheriff to have you around. I want you to know that."

"Thanks, Seth." Raaven looked a bit self-consciously at her half-eaten plate. "I guess I'm going to have to tell you more strange tales if that's the reaction I get."

"No. You keep doing the job you do for Custer County and me. That'll do it. And, speaking of that, I guess we've taken a long enough break from that pile of work."

"Yeah, I suppose we have," Raaven said as she scooted along the bench towards the end of the table.

Before she could stand up, the sheriff said, "Oh, one other question. Would you like to have your black hair back again?"

Raaven turned back about half-way, "Not sure about the hair, but I would like to get back that spirit that was lost all those years ago. I hate to think it is lost and maybe searching for me. You know, Indians are kind of funny about things such as that. Kind of funny."

"Yeah, I know," the sheriff nodded his recognition.

Raaven stood up, and as Sheriff Ironwood moved to stand, she added. "And, I'd like to get my sister back with it."

✝

BLOOD SILENCE

Peering into the abyss

I T WAS AS SILENT in the room as if all in the space was a vacuum; as if the lack of air prevented the vibrations of sound from reaching the waiting human eardrum. The sheriff looked first at Simon Peter Straw and then at his deputy, but the lawman refused to speak; just as the suspect he was attempting to question had done for nearly twenty minutes. It was a standoff, and the only sounds that penetrated the noiselessness of the room were those that drifted from down the hall and bounced about the sheriff's office unchallenged. The sheriff seemed to pay no attention to the routine noises of his department as he sat still with a look of stern resolution on his face.

Deputy Stark, too, was motionless. She sat on the edge of her chair with her hands folded in her lap cradling a small notebook. Like the sheriff, she stared intently at Simon Peter who remained still and quiet as a statue. His features seemed to be chiseled stone rather than flesh, and his dark Indian eyes were fixed like lasers on the corner of the sheriff's desk. Seth Ironwood knew what the young man was looking at. He had placed it there deliberately because he reasoned that the small stone owl, faded green in shade, now sitting on that corner with its miniature beak and great round eyes directed at the detainee, was somehow special to the man. The sheriff had taken it from the confiscated belongings of the suspect; and although he wasn't sure what meaning it carried, he was sure that the small amulet meant something. Finally, the sheriff abruptly broke the stillness with a calculated sternness in his voice.

"All right, Simon P, have it your way. But, before I return you to your accommodations, let me ask you one more time. Where is your brother? We believe your brother is holding Alex Austenne against his will. We don't know what he plans to do with the Custer reenactor; but, if it is what I think it is, you don't want to be a part of that. Because, that will mean you will be an accessory to a very serious crime; if that's what your brother does. And, Simon, in this state that also means you will be as guilty as he; and, young man, you will have the same toxic chemicals run through your veins until you are dead, as will be your brother Andrew. The Straw twins will suffer the same fate as the man they kill. In that case, Simon P, no one wins a thing: except the devil."

Sheriff Ironwood paused as he reached out and retrieved the stone owl and glanced towards the deputy. Raaven Stark didn't return his look but kept her gaze fixed on Simon. She saw his eyes finally show life, as they stared intently toward the sheriff's hand as Ironwood made the small stone bird disappear in the folds of his long bony fingers.

"Simon, listen to me carefully," the deputy interrupted. "I have Indian blood like you. I think I know what your code is telling you to do. I'm not sure I wouldn't do the very same if I found myself in your place. But, let me also say this to you. What your brother is about to do will stain the waters of the Washita River no different than what General Custer did so many years ago."

She waited for just a second to see if that caught Simon's attention. It did. He at last turned his head and his gaze to meet the eyes of Deputy Stark, and she took energy from the dark stare that met hers.

"And that stain," she continued her plea, "like the stain of the blood of Black Kettle did then, will also wash to the sea now. There it too will mingle with the ancestors just as the peace chief's had done all those years ago. But this time, Simon, the spirits will be the ancestors of your ancient enemy. And at some future, maybe very distant time from now, in a place far from us; those ancestors' children will return to you the oath of revenge. But this time, it will be with revenge of their own. They will renew the cycle. It is a cycle, Simon, which never can end. Don't you see that?"

Simon stared for a long second at the deputy, and then he turned towards Sheriff Ironwood.

Staring at the floor just in front of his chair, he said. "I have taken an oath with my brother. I cannot betray my oath."

Ironwood resisted the impulse to jump on this first admission with a quick question. He waited and slowly pushed his tall frame forward in his chair. He rested his elbows on his desk and looked intently at Simon Peter. Finally, the sheriff extended his hand, the one with the small stone piece in it, toward the suspect. As he did, he could see Simon stiffen slightly with his eyes now fixed on that hand that held the owl.

The sheriff opened his fingers slowly, palm up so that the green object caught the light from the overhead.

"Does this little fellow have anything to do with that oath?" The sheriff waited.

Simon Peter merely looked at the amulet for a moment.

"Yes," he said finally, dropping his gaze to his lap. "It is the oath." Simon Peter then turned his eyes toward Deputy Stark.

"It is the oath of justice my brother and I swore to when we were teenagers; when we were at Saint Joseph's Indian School. It is the *Oath of the Jade Owl*."

"Simon P," the sheriff responded with a tone that was both soft and stern, "if I give this piece of stone back to you, will you tell me the story?"

Simon hesitated, but then looked toward the deputy. As he did he dropped his eyes and murmured. "Yes."

Sheriff Ironwood held out his hand across the desk with the small green owl in his open palm. Simon, without hesitation, took the warm piece of stone; and, as the sheriff had done, made it disappear from sight in his fist. The silence returned to the room.

✝

MESSAGE IN A BOTTLE

Blood is thicker than whiskey

S HERIFF IRONWOOD got up from his desk and slowly made his way to the office door. He closed it quietly. The sheriff's staff knew not to come through that door when it was closed, so he shut it. The sheriff returned to his desk, and sat down; he let his back push the chair into a comfortable angle. As usual, he looked up at the dingy ceiling just above his desk. Uninvited, the thought came to mind that he would have to talk to the cleaning crew about that ceiling. Then returning his gaze to the room, he first glanced at Deputy Stark and then swiftly diverted his eyes to the man he was trying to understand; Simon Peter Straw.

"Okay, son, anytime you're ready, I'm ready to hear it."

Simon Peter opened his fingers slightly and stared at the stone figurine before he spoke. At last, without looking up at the sheriff, he began.

"Like I said before, Sheriff, it all started at the Indian school in South Dakota. Andy and I had been there for nearly three years. Our mom had put us in the Catholic school to keep our old man from beating us, which he did when he got drunk; and he got drunk almost every night. He wasn't our real dad, but we never knew him. Carl was all we ever knew. He was more a white man than an Indian; at least that's what he always bragged about.

"He was sort of unusual in that way. Most Indians wanted to run away from any mixed blood they had. It shamed them. Not old Carl. When he got drunk he would shout for the whole world to hear that he was glad the whites had nearly wiped out all those savages. And when he said savages the word came out like he had said nigger. Carl had more than one fight over it too. But it never turned him. As soon as he got drunk he'd start all over with it. It scared me and my brother. It scared us a lot.

"I remember this one time real good. It was just before we came to the St. Joseph's School. Mom was gone somewhere, probably to the grocery. Andy and I were left alone with Carl. He'd been drinking all day and could hardly stand up. Andy decided he would play a trick on the stupid fool. I begged him not to, but he wouldn't listen. I told him that Carl would beat us for sure if he found out.

"But my brother peed in Carl's whiskey bottle anyway, while the big man had gone to the bathroom. The bottle was nearly empty, but when Andy finished it was nearly half full. The color was a bit more yellow, but it still looked like Jack.

"Carl never even noticed. He was so drunk he just filled his glass with the piss and whiskey. He always drank the stuff straight too. *He didn't like to mix his juice,* he said. It was all we could do not to laugh when we saw that bastard drinking from that bottle. Carl never let on nothing either. He just kept drinking that stuff. What was so funny is he seemed to really like it. We just stared at each other, trying not to break up.

"But then he started in on us again, like he always did. He said what he always said to us too. He called us *Custer killers*. He said it was our kind that had killed that great soldier at the Little Big Horn. He almost screamed, *that if them savages hadn't killed the general, he'd have wiped out the whole dirty bunch of you before he was done.*

"Andy and I just held our tongue and watched him drink my brother's urine. We prayed he'd pass out. That way he wouldn't hit us.

"At that time, we lived just outside the reservation in an old mobile home that was mostly junk. It had belonged to my real father and was so old that some of the metal siding had peeled away so as you could see the ragged insulation. The hot-water heater was exposed to the elements and was rusting something awful. Andy I would take bets on how long it would take before it busted a gut, and there would be nothing but cold showers after that. It was all we ever knew, until we got sent to the Indian school. What a blessing that was even though me and Andy couldn't see it at the time.

"Andy and I are identical twins. We looked so much alike that we had a lot of fun fooling people about which one we were. We were in our mid-teens and seemed to enjoy making trouble at the school. Father Ignacio, who ran that show, tried to steer us right but both of us resisted that path; it was too much fun going the other way. It was a wonder that we didn't get kicked out of St. Joseph's. But we didn't. The father always gave us penance to do after confession and let us go on until the next time. He was one patient man, I can tell you that."

Simon Peter stopped his monologue and glanced at the deputy for a moment, she was busy taking notes. Then he met directly the eyes of Sheriff Ironwood. The young man paused for so long that the sheriff began to think he wasn't going to continue. But, finally, he again looked at the amulet cradled in his hand before he started.

"The owl thing started about two weeks before we were to graduate from the high school," he said softly. "We had a celebration powwow at the school to raise money from donors for the graduation ceremony and for some scholarship money for a couple of the students. The father had told me that I might get some help going on to community college, if that's what I wanted. Andy's grades weren't good enough for that so he had decided to go into the army. He had already signed up and was scheduled to go to boot camp right after graduation. The army had given him a small bonus for enlisting, and Andy and I were looking forward to the big party we were going to have with that money before Andy shipped out to basic.

"One night in our dorm room, after the dancing around the sacred fire earlier that evening, my brother and I turned out the lights and started talking about our ancestors in the darkened room. Andy had a small leather bag around his neck, he called it his spirit bag, and from it he took a button and we shared it. We both were full of the excitement from the dancing and wanted to have a vision; you know, like our bloods used to do.

"Andy said he wanted to talk to the spirit of the Chief. I thought he meant Black Kettle, but as we got high and talked more, strange images came to us. That's when I knew he meant Blood Feather, the Cheyenne Dog Soldier from so long ago. He was the great-great grandfather of our mother. Andy said that's who he wanted to be like. He said that when he got into the army he would train hard so that he could become a Ranger and be a great warrior. He said he would become a Dog Soldier in his heart; in his spirit. He said that the whites would never know it, but that's what he would be.

"Then he said something really strange, even for Andy. He said when he came home from the army, he would revenge the death of Black Kettle, our ancestor of the ancient Cheyenne. I remember I responded to my brother's notion with a big grin. Andy flashed an angry look back at me. It was then I understood for the first time that he was serious; deadly serious.

"I couldn't believe what he was saying. I tried to reason with him. I told him it was impossible to revenge the death of someone that lived over a hundred fifty years ago. I tried to explain to my brother that their spirits are all long dead and gone. No one remembers them outside the history books; probably not even their relatives. I remember he looked at me for a long time in a way that I had never seen before. The anger was gone but his stare was intense. Even in the darkened room with only a small candle burning, I knew Andy had something very heavy hanging on his soul. He didn't speak for a long time. He just fingered something in his hand and stared at it. I couldn't see what it was, but I thought I knew what was coming.

"*What about your ancestors?* he finally said. *Do you remember them?* But, before I could answer, he added. *And do you remember this?*

"He extended his hand like I am doing to you now; as he did he slowly unfolded his fingers and showed me what he was holding."

Simon Peter held up the jade colored owl between his thumb and forefinger so the sheriff could see it.

"I hesitated because I knew what he meant. *Well...well,* I said finally, *sure I remember them Andy. But that's not the same.*

"*Why not?* he said in a soft but hard voice. *How can you say they're gone and forgotten. You know what our mother always said about her people, our people; you remember, don't you?*

"*Well sure, I remember. She said they were right here with us. Always with us. I remember that well.*

"*And she said something else too, didn't she? I mean about what we owed to them. What did she say, Simon?*

"*You mean about their spirits?*

"*Yeah,* Andy said as he again made the owl vanish in his hand.

"I answered, *Mother said we should always think about restoring the honor to our people. But, Andy, I never knew what she meant by that. Did you?*

"*I didn't then, but I do now. I know exactly what she meant. Weird as it is, it was Carl that finally made me see that; made me see that a wrong is always a wrong until it is righted. Time doesn't make a wrong right, Simon. Time only makes the memory fade for most people. Justice is eternal. If you got anything out of this white man's school and the old father, you got that. Right?*

"After that we both just sat still in the dark. When Andy didn't say anything else, I began to think he was just playing a game with me. He was the kind who liked to make a mystery out of everything. You know, lead you on. Play a trick on you and then laugh when you found out the joke was on you. He loved the game, especially if he was the only one who really understood the rules. My brother wasn't book smart, but he was smart in other ways; especially in the ways of the Indian; the spirit ways.

"Then finally Andy said, *She meant that we must restore the honor to Black Kettle...we must find a way to bring justice finally to his spirit; the spirit that was wounded at Sand Creek and the body that was killed and left to float on that cold water in November on the Washita River in Indian Territory. Black Kettle has been lost for all of these years, and there is only one way to give him peace. I'm telling you, Simon, there's only one way.*"

Simon Peter stopped his narrative and again peered intently at the small stone in his hand. To the sheriff and Deputy Stark, waiting patiently for him to continue, it appeared that Simon was taking the story directly from the stone.

"Simon P," the sheriff finally broke the quiet, "tell me about the oath you boys swore that day. Can you do that?"

Simon Peter seemed to relax a bit in his chair. "Sheriff, do you think I could have some water?"

"Sure. Deputy, can you do that for us?"

"I can, Sheriff; be right back."

The two men sat still while they waited for Deputy Stark to return. Sheriff Ironwood looked at Simon while the young man continued to keep his own eyes focused on his hand. The sheriff found himself liking this Indian. He suddenly, as he looked across the desk, felt responsible for these two Straw men. He shivered slightly as a slight vibration passed involuntarily through his body. As he did the deputy returned and again closed the door before she handed the bottled water to Simon. He drank eagerly and finished off the contents before handing the empty plastic container back to the deputy.

"Like I told you, we called it the *Oath of the Jade Owl*," he said as he nodded a thank you to the deputy for the water.

"Andy made it up. I remember thinking when he told me about it that my brother was a whole lot smarter than his grades at St. Joseph showed. He was a thinker, a deep thinker; that much was obvious to me."

Simon turned once again to look at Raaven Stark before he went on.

"Deputy, do you believe that Indians have a different kind of spirit than the white man? I mean do Indian people see things that white people don't?"

"What kind of things, Simon? I'm not sure I understand your question."

Simon Peter didn't answer for a moment, but then he spoke slowly and so softly that the deputy had to lean forward in her chair to hear him.

"My brother said that Indian people can see the spirit of a man, but that white people can't. He said that for Indians, if they are going to kill a man they knew that they have to kill him twice."

Deputy Stark gave a quick glance toward the sheriff before she answered.

"Kill him twice; is that what you said, Simon?"

"Yeah. Andy said that an Indian knows that if you only kill the body that the spirit will escape, and some day you will be sorry. You'll have to kill the body and the spirit at the same time or that spirit will come back for its revenge. It will come back in a different body, and you won't recognize it until it's too late.

"That's why Indians in the old days always mutilated the corpse. You know like cutting off their heads and feet; and, well you know; their private parts. The body was already dead, so why do that? They did it to kill the spirit. To kill the man twice so he would never come back for revenge or justice."

The room behind the closed door fell silent for a moment. Sheriff Ironwood again took the initiative.

"Simon, has this got something to do with the oath you boys took? This killing a man twice notion?"

"Yeah, Sheriff. That's what the oath is all about. Andy said that when Custer killed Black Kettle on the Washita River he really didn't kill him twice. He only killed his body; that was all. Black Kettle's spirit escaped. He said, too, that Black Kettle's son Blood Feather was the same. The soldiers of the Seventh Cavalry never killed his spirit. Andy told me he believed that his distant grandfather's spirit was in him. It was in him and wanted Andy to bring justice for the wrong that Custer had done to his people."

"Is that what Andy is about now?"

Simon hesitated for a moment, "Yes. He's going to kill General Custer. It won't be long from now either. Andy has him. I'm sure. We had made plans all along on how to get him. How to recognize him."

"Simon, you'll have to forgive an old, slow sheriff, but I don't get it. George Armstrong Custer, the commander of the Seventh Cavalry, has been dead since that day at the Little Big Horn; when was it? 1870 something."

"1876, in July," the deputy interrupted.

"Yeah, that's it, Stark, thank you. Anyway, I know this much son; oath or no oath, that crusty old soldier was made into dust years and years ago. Now I also know that you Indians have a little different take on such things as us whites, but I don't think that changes the physics of the matter very much. The only place you're going to find old Custer is in the history books. You understand me?"

Simon Peter looked at Raaven Stark as if to ask her for help. The deputy returned his glance, and then she turned to the sheriff.

"Sheriff, I think I can add something here if you'll permit me."

Ironwood appeared a bit surprised by the interruption. "Well, Deputy, if you can move us along here, by all means, be my guest."

"I think what Simon is trying to tell you, Seth, is that you're right as far as it goes. Custer is certainly dead and gone to cosmic dust, but there's a catch."

"A catch? Stark."

"Yeah. You see, when the Sioux of Sitting Bull's band and the Cheyenne attacked and wiped out Custer and his men of the Seventh at the Little Big Horn on that hot summer day in July, they only got it half-right when it came to the general. I don't know how much of the historical account you know, but after the Indians had killed all the soldiers on the hill, the women set about to mutilate the bodies. This was their way of destroying the spirit for the afterlife. What the rescue cavalry found later was a horrendous scene of unrecognizable and, in many cases, scattered pieces of the soldiers who had fought there. That is, with one remarkable exception."

Deputy Stark paused and met the eyes of Simon Peter. She nodded, and he returned the gesture to indicate recognition of the story she was telling.

"Custer's body was intact," she continued. "The only thing the Indian women had done to it was puncture his eardrums with a sewing awl. Some say it was so he would hear better in the afterlife. You see Custer had long ignored the warnings of Indians who had told him that if he attacked them again, they meant in reference to the Washita River incident, he would lose his life. You see Custer wasn't scalped or beheaded. His genitals were still in their normal place. His eyes had not been touched; his feet were still firmly attached to his ankles. Custer, in other words, in all his magnificence was still Custer with one exception."

"Yeah," the sheriff interrupted. "He was dead as a doorknob. Right?"

"So to speak, Seth."

"So to speak?"

"Well, yes, Sheriff, that's the point that Simon is trying to make. General Custer's body was dead, but…"

Again Ironwood cut in. "But…his spirit was still around; was somehow flying about free as a bird. That's it?"

"That's it, Seth. And, to Simon here and his brother, that spirit is still floating around after over one hundred fifty years. Did I get that right, Simon?"

The young man slowly nodded his agreement.

Sheriff Ironwood leaned back in his chair; again he looked at the dirty ceiling tiles.

"Okay then. I've only got one more question, Simon." The sheriff returned his chair square to the floor and leaned on his elbows over his desk. He looked intently at the young man for a moment.

"Where's your brother?"

Simon Peter lowered his eyes once again to his folded hands in his lap.

"I can't tell you, Sheriff," he said faintly. "I swore I wouldn't. He's my brother, and we took an oath; a blood oath."

Sheriff Ironwood again leaned back. As he did, the door slowly cracked and the dispatcher Taylor Bebe, warily stuck only his head through the opening.

"Sheriff, I'm sorry to interrupt, but there's a Father Juan Bosco here to see you. He says he has an appointment."

The sheriff pushed his chair back and headed for the door.

"Don't anybody go anywhere; I'll be right back," he said as he eased out the door and shut it behind him.

Deputy Stark waited for a moment after the sheriff's exit before she spoke.

"Simon, I want to tell you something while the sheriff is out of the room: just one Indian to another. Okay?"

Simon Peter looked at the deputy but didn't answer, so she continued.

"You asked me earlier about seeing spirits; about whether an Indian can see spirits that the white man can't. The short answer, Simon, is that I believe they can. Indians have always spoken with the spirits. That's one of the fundamental differences between our people and the white man. For them it is reason that is primary; for us, it is the mystery of the Great Creation that is most important to our culture. For us the spirits of all our ancestors float around us all the time. They are there to help us navigate through this very difficult world. You know that already. But where you and your brother are wrong is about the killing. Simon, you can't kill a spirit any more than you can grab its hand. A spirit is like the wind; all around us to be felt, but not there to be seen or touched. We know it is there not by seeing it, but by what it does to us. How it makes us act. It's like how the wind can knock you down, but you never see it. It's there, yet it's not there. Do you see my point, Simon?"

The young man sat motionless as he had during most of the interview. "Yes, I see your point," he said quietly. "I know you're right, too. So does Andy. But what you don't understand, Deputy Stark, is what we mean by killing the spirit. But you will soon enough; soon enough you will know."

Raaven Stark was about to press for an explanation when the door opened and Sheriff Ironwood eased back into the room. Without speaking he returned to his desk. As he passed Simon Peter the sheriff laid his hand on Simon's shoulder for an instant. Simon Peter reacted by looking up at the sheriff and watching him as the tall man settled into his chair and leaned back and looked up at the ceiling.

Without lowering his gaze he said, "Okay, where were we?"

✝

DOWN BY THE RIVER

New water running over old souls

ALEX FELT the rude push from behind in the middle of his back. It was just with enough force to make him stumble slightly, and he cussed under his breath. His hands were cuffed awkwardly behind his neck and a small-linked chain ran from the middle of the cuffs down to his military belt. The trail was obscure, but the path was smooth and uncluttered; it was surely a finished and well-kept surface Alex reasoned. He wanted to turn around and face his abductor, but the man pushing him along had made it clear he was not to either turn around or hesitate. So Alex Austenne did as he was told; he was not a brave man.

In spite of his circumstance, the fantastic thought suddenly came to him that the Indians had made him captive in order to seek revenge for his campaign against them. He wondered what his superior officers would think of him; allowing, as he had, to be taken into the hands of the heathen enemy. Alex couldn't help but grin slightly as he realized how easy it was for him to move from Alex to the *General*: from a moment in the real time to a moment in fantasy. He had played the *General* for so long that it was no longer an act. He was Custer as much as he was Austenne; maybe more so. Alex often relied on the story of Dr. Henry Jekyll and Mr. Edward Hyde to describe to those who asked what it was like to be George Armstrong Custer in the first person. Alex was always careful to explain the transition was not from the good to the evil as in Stevenson's tale, but rather from the mundane to the sublime: from the world of the ordinary to the world of the heroic, a world that most men wanted to inhabit, but very few ever did or could.

The Custer reenactor knew one thing for sure; he liked his life more when he was the *General*. Alex had long suspected that Jane also preferred her husband when he was in costume, both inside and out. It was true, Alex was a different man when he took on the character of the 19th century Indian fighting cavalry officer; it was just a great place to be.

Often, in the exhilaration that stayed with him long after the performance, Alex would discover himself aroused. Jane always seemed to catch the scent as well and the two would make love; it was always the best. There was a special kind of passion between the two as the *General* pulled off his military uniform and tossed the brass buttons in a pile on the floor; it was more lust than love-making, more animal than human. Damn fun. Alex loved the invented. At those moments, he conjured orders from Fort Leavenworth; orders to move out onto the plains with the dawn of the morrow, orders from General Sheridan to begin the hunt for the Cheyenne and the Lakota. His make-believe with his beloved never failed to stir him deeply. The game that gave fate a central role in their lives always attended to heighten the desire between the lovers. In the quiet and still that followed, the *General*, with an affectation that was both quiet and tender, would call his wife *his little Libbie*, and she never scolded her *gallant*, as she called her husband in return.

The sweetness of the recollection was ousted as Alex felt his kidnapper's hand touch his back again, pushing him along the trail, and pushing the *General* from Alex's thoughts. The slight shove brought him back to the moment rudely, to the reality of the unknown and the darkness that blunted all his senses of time and place.

Alex's awkwardly elevated right arm was beginning to become numb so he flexed his fingers rhythmically, attempting to encourage the natural circulation. Abruptly the trail veered to the right, and the captive could just make out in the distance the reflection of moonlight on water. He wasn't sure if it was a pond or lake or river, but he could see that the two on the trail were soon to be halted by it.

Whatever the stranger that pushed him along on this trail in the dark wanted, whatever was going to happen, Alex thought, he would soon learn. The small granite pebbles crunched under the feet of the two as they moved along. The noise they gave off created a syncopated rhythm that reminded Alex of his marching days in the military. As they came close to the water, he thought about his wife again. He suspected that she would be in a panic not knowing what the sudden, uncustomary interruption meant. He said a silent plea that she would figure something was wrong, and notify the authorities.

But then Alex wondered what she would say to them.

What could she tell them? She wouldn't even know for sure that something was wrong. How could she? All she could go on was the sudden dead phone: her husband laughing about the outburst at his presentation one moment, and the next, only silence.

The trail again veered sharply. Alex could just make out a table or bench directly in front of them. It appeared to be the kind that is a fixture in most public parks. As he came to the immovable mass of concrete he was forced to stop.

"Take a seat, *General*," the voice from behind said with a calmness that seemed out of place to Alex.

Alex reluctantly, with only a slight hesitation, pushed one leg over the bench seat, and then the other. He put his elbows on the hard surface and waited, again flexing his elevated hand. While his captor moved to the opposite side of the table, Alex tried to peer through the darkness. There was a slight hint of new light coming into the sky, so at least now he knew which way was east.

He squinted hoping to catch any detail he could. That's when he saw what looked like a contraption of some sort on an adjacent table. Alex's first notion of the object was of some type of pipe that appeared to be mounted and secured on a stand. He was sure of one thing; it pointed in his direction.

"Relax, *General*. We'll wait a bit until the light comes before we begin. Just relax. I'm not going to hurt you unless you force me to."

Alex sensed the apprehension that he had felt since he was taken prisoner give way to one of anger. He violently jerked at his at cuffs and chain that bound him.

"I don't know who you are or what you want, but I do

know that this is one damn sick game you're playing. Take these fuckin' cuffs off me! And I'm not *General*...my name is Alex Austenne," Alex barked.

The demand was met with silence so Alex tried again. "Okay...let me go right now, and I give you my word that I will simply walk out of here. I won't press charges; I'll just forget this ever happened. Got it? We'll just chalk this up to one very bad joke. Okay?" The only response Alex got came from some distant bird beginning its call in celebration of the approaching new day. The stranger across the concrete top of the bench said nothing.

✝

WALKING WITH COWS

The well-worn path to nowhere

"SIMON, ARE YOU familiar with cows?"

"Yes, I guess so. My mom's brother owned a ranch in South Dakota. Andy and I used to stay with him some."

"Have you ever watched cows as they make their way from one place to another?" the sheriff continued.

"I don't know; never thought about it..."

"Well when cows move in distance they always follow a well-worn path. In other words, they take the path of least resistance, and the one most familiar. And, they will do this no matter what. A few years ago I raised a small herd over by Cheyenne. I had them on about two hundred acres, and every now and then I would move their watering trough so that they would go into different paddocks to graze. That's when I noticed that no matter where I moved the water, the cows would always return down the same path to where the water trough had been. Of course, once there, they would usually strike out for the water in its new location.

"But the point is that they moved along this familiar path without thinking where they were going. It didn't matter. They just knew the path and that was it. So they took it.

"You see, all dumb animals do much the same. They don't make choices about their future; where they're going or what will happen when they get there. They move by instinct; in the case of the herd, the instinct that this well-worn path will take them to water; even if it leads them to a dry hole.

"The message, Simon, is that what you are doing with your oath is very much like what dumb animals do by instinct. You're moving on a well-worn path that has been followed without thinking for all of man's existence. That path is called revenge. You want an eye-for-an-eye. And that notion of revenge is taking you down a path that is familiar and easy, but is also taking you to someplace, I can promise you, that you really don't want to go.

"You must understand, Simon, revenge is a very ugly thing when it is actually carried out. It is exactly the opposite of what you say you are after. Revenge is not the same as justice, Simon. But, don't take my word for it. I've got someone here that I want you to listen to. I think he will do a better job at making the case."

Sheriff Ironwood hovered over his desk and hit the intercom button on the phone. "Bebe, would you escort my guest to my office, please?"

The sheriff leaned back in his chair and waited for his door to open. He was anticipating, and anxious to see the reaction of Simon.

As Father Juan Bosco followed the dispatcher through the door, the sheriff stood up and came around his desk to greet him. Simon Peter sat still and didn't turn around in his chair to see who had entered the office, but as the sheriff spoke his greeting to the priest, Ironwood noticed out of the corner of his eye that Simon straightened in his seat.

"Father, I want you to meet someone." The sheriff led the Catholic priest around to face Simon Peter.

Without hesitation the father spoke. "Simon, Sheriff Ironwood tells me you are from St. Joseph's Indian School. Is that right?" The father extended his hand deliberately, as if greeting an old friend.

At first he got no response, but then Simon looked up and met the bright dark eyes of the Jesuit holy man. He accepted the handshake, but didn't respond to the question.

The sheriff quickly positioned a chair close and motioned for the father to take a seat.

"You know," Father Juan continued as he sat, "I once worked with Father Ignacio when we both were a part of the same archdiocese in St. Louis. I have long admired his devotion to the work he does among the Native Americans of South Dakota. If I remember him well, he was a very patient and caring man. Am I right?"

Father Juan again waited for a response, but the silence, as always, made the room seem smaller than it was.

"Yes, Father, he was more than that," Simon said quietly without gesture as he looked up and met the gaze of the priest. "He was our best friend. Andy and me. He baptized us both in the church. He meant a lot to us; he was the only real father we ever had."

"That's very good to hear, Simon. Sometimes we, as clergy, don't know whether our message gets through, especially to the young people in our care. Yes, that's good to hear." Father Juan sat more erect in his chair and slid slightly forward in the seat. He nodded quickly to the sheriff before he continued.

"Simon, the sheriff tells me that you and your brother have taken some sort of oath of revenge; is that right?"

Simon Peter abruptly stood up without warning as if he had been touched with a hot iron rod. He turned to face Father Juan directly. The sheriff and the deputy both tensed in their chairs, but neither one rose from their seats, they just watched the drama.

Simon Peter stared down at the father for a moment, and then spoke, "It is not an oath of revenge; it is an oath to bring justice for what was done." The word justice came from his lips as a restrained shout. "Justice that has always been denied my people."

Father Juan didn't flinch at the outburst; he simply remained quiet in his chair, but he never took his eyes off the man standing over him. He was about to respond when the sheriff beat him to it.

"Okay, Simon. We get it, but maybe it would be better if you sat back down. It could be that this is what we need to understand better." The sheriff waited for his message to take effect. Without another word, Simon Peter sat down and stared at his clinched fist in his lap.

Father Juan took the opportunity to try again.

"Justice and revenge; these are difficult ideas to grasp sometimes, Simon. Even in my business, I have a hard time understanding the difference at times. Often they get switched about with the circumstances that give rise to the need to consider one or the other as a course of action."

The father looked at the sheriff as he continued.

"You say your oath with your brother is about seeking justice for an ancient wrong, and the sheriff here seems to think it is an oath about revenging that wrong perpetrated by the troops of General Custer's Seventh Cavalry done to your ancestors so many years ago. Maybe it could help us prevent another wrong being done, if we could understand which of you is closest to the truth. Why don't you tell me about the oath? Tell me what you and Andrew swore to one another those years ago at St. Joseph's."

Simon switched his eyes from the priest and looked at Deputy Stark. "She can tell you," he said. "I want her to tell you. She is an Indian like me; like my brother."

Both men looked at the deputy simultaneously. The sheriff spoke to her in an inquisitive tone. "What's going on, Raaven?"

"I'm not sure, Sheriff. Simon and I had a little conversation while you were out of the office." Deputy Stark leaned forward in her chair. She looked for a long moment at Simon Peter.

"Okay, I think they're after the spirit of Custer. I think that's it in a nutshell." The deputy continued to meet Simon Peter's stare, and he returned her look with a slight nod.

"They want to kill the old general's spirit; they think it is still around after all these years, and Chief Black Kettle will have no peace until they do." Raaven first looked at the sheriff, and then she turned toward Father Juan.

The priest glanced at the sheriff briefly before he responded to what he had heard.

"That makes sense to me," Father Juan said quietly. "The Catholic Church has long taught of the spirits among us. Simon, I'm sure you heard Father Ignacio speak often of the presence of the Saints, helping us through this life. And, I know you remember well the many times in the Mass when we pray for the spirits of the departed loved ones who are no longer with us in their physical bodies, but are with us in the spirit. And then there are the visions. The history of our faith is full of them in all of the two thousand years since Saul was knocked off his horse by the most powerful spirit that has ever existed. Right? You remember that story? I'm sure you do, Simon."

Father Juan paused for a moment.

"I remember," Simon Peter said softly.

"Well then, I think we can agree on that; but, Simon, there is something we cannot agree on. Young man, spirits are eternal by the Grace of God. You cannot destroy them; they belong to God, not to this world. I'm sure you see that. Am I right?"

There was no response from Simon Peter; he sat still staring intently at his closed fist.

Father Juan looked first at the sheriff and then at Deputy Stark. He gave a shrug to both. Then he turned back to face Simon Peter.

"Okay, Simon. We'll leave that for now. But let's talk about seeking justice or revenge, or whatever you think you will accomplish by your oath. I'm going to tell you what I think is the difference between the two, and I want you to tell me which one best describes what you and Andy are about. Okay? Will you at least do that for me?" The father relaxed in his chair and waited.

Simon Peter finally looked up at the priest, and only nodded before lowering his eyes once again to his clinched fist.

"Okay then. You remember, I'm sure, Simon, some of the lessons from the Old Testament you learned at St. Joseph's. One of those lessons, I suspect, had to be about what was considered justice in the times of the Hebrews. For example, in the book of Exodus you read the words *But if there is serious injury, you are to take life for life, eye for eye, tooth for tooth, hand for hand, foot for foot.* And in Leviticus it is written that *The one who inflicted the injury must suffer the same injury.* And again in Deuteronomy, justice is judged to be like for like, as it teaches to *Show no pity. You must purge from Israel the guilt of shedding innocent blood, so that it may go well with you.*

"So it's clear in those passages what justice in our world means or, at least, what it meant over two thousand years ago. That is how you are to go about setting a wrong right; righting a wrong done to someone or even to a people. To put it plainly, the message is, *I will take your eye if you take mine.* Pretty clear and simple, wouldn't you say, Simon?"

Father Juan paused, anticipating a reaction, but there was none so he continued.

"But then something happened to change the rules, and I think you know well what that was. His name was Jesus; Christ Jesus, the Son of God. And the new meaning of justice came with Him in His teachings; in His actions while He lived among us. That new rule of justice is probably captured best in the Gospel of Matthew when the author writes that *You have heard that it was said, 'An eye for an eye, and a tooth for a tooth.' But I say to you, do not resist an evil person; but whoever slaps you on your right cheek, turn the other to him also...*

"That's what we might call in today's terms, Simon, a real game-changer: wouldn't you agree? And, there's one other little modification to the old rule which has turned the whole idea of justice on its ear. It's captured in Romans in the New Testament.

Never take your own revenge, beloved, but leave room for the wrath of God, for it is written, 'Vengeance is Mine, I will repay,' says the Lord.

"So, what we have to understand is that the ancient definition of justice from the Old Testament is turned into what we would call now, revenge. You do me a hurt, I will do you likewise. And, revenge is so easy to understand in our culture. So many of the most popular movies use this theme, and we can't help ourselves but always hope for *sweet revenge* to befall the villain at the hands of the avenging good guy.

"But the new rule asks us to do something else that is so very hard for us to do when we suffer a wrong. That something else is also in that verse from Romans in the New Testament.

"*But if your enemy is hungry, feed him, and if he is thirsty, give him a drink; for in so doing you will heap burning coals on his head. Do not overcome by evil, but overcome evil with good.*"

Father Juan again stopped. He looked at Sheriff Ironwood, but didn't offer a change of expression. Then he turned back to Simon Peter. The priest reached out and put his hand gently on the man's forearm.

"You see, Simon, it's not really too hard to understand. Revenge is when I take your eye, because you have taken mine. Justice is when we let God take it for us. The final take on this difference is that God's justice always points to the future; something better. Revenge always points to the past, and the same old cycle of hurt for hurt. God's justice always calls for forgiveness, and by doing so frees us from hate. Revenge does just the opposite; it always traps us in a vicious cycle; the ancient eye for an eye, Simon, only makes us blind, never satisfied with a notion of justice."

Father Juan relaxed and waited.

Sheriff Ironwood swiveled his chair forward and rested his elbows on his desk. He looked intently at Simon Peter.

"Simon, are you going to help us? No, are you going to help yourself and your brother, and tell us where he is and what he is doing with Mr. Austenne?"

At last Simon Peter looked up and met the sheriff's gaze. He then turned to the priest.

"Father, you know earlier you said that a spirit cannot be killed."

"Yes I did. God has made the spirit and only He can change that. It is eternal."

Simon Peter paused for a moment, and a very slight smile moved his lips.

"I believe that too, and so does Andy. We both understand that teaching of our faith. We understand it well. That is why we have taken our oath. We know that the spirit of our ancient grandfather is still around us. He has long waited for what you say is God's justice, and so have we.

And the spirit of General George Armstrong Custer is also still around. And, he is due that same justice. That is what my brother is doing now. He is trying to bring that justice to our grandfather now, while we are on this earth; before we become spirits ourselves. It is something we must do; we both know that as true."

The sheriff spoke with an edge to his voice.

"Simon, enough! It is time we get somewhere. Is Andy going to hurt Alex Austenne?"

Simon Peter sat straight in his chair. "No. He will not hurt Mr. Austenne, but…"

"But what?" the sheriff interjected forcefully.

"He will see to it that the spirit that he carries with him; the spirit of the General, will condemn itself for all eternity. That spirit will at last find God's justice."

Simon Peter diverted his eyes to Father Juan and repeated. "That spirit will damn itself, and will trouble my people no more."

"Where is Andy, Simon? If you do not tell me now, I am going to have to charge you. Do you understand? And I've got a whole list…." Suddenly the sheriff stopped in mid-sentence and stood up behind his desk. To the others in the room, especially Raaven Stark, Sheriff Ironwood's appearance was strange in the extreme. The man stood as if he was made of stone; as if he was suddenly made a statue, rigid and cold.

As the deputy rose from her chair to speak to the sheriff, Ironwood spoke.

"Never mind, Simon; I know exactly where he is. What's wrong with me? I've known all along." The sheriff circled to the front of his desk and nodded toward Deputy Stark. He gave a slight wink at her as he simultaneously extended his hand to Father Juan.

"Thanks, Father. You have been a great help." Ironwood then turned to Deputy Stark. "Get your Jeep and come to the front of the station. You and I and our young friend here are going to see Andrew Straw and Alex Austenne."

As Father Juan was about to leave just ahead of Deputy Stark, the sheriff called after him.

"Wait a minute, Father; hold on for a sec. I want you to hear this." Sheriff Ironwood then looked intently at Simon Peter.

"Son, I know now; suddenly I know what you have been doing all along."

As the sheriff paused to let the message sink in, Simon Peter stood up to face the lawman. He smiled almost imperceptibly before he extended his hand and opened his fist. Without a word he handed the jade owl back to the sheriff, and then he glanced quickly toward the priest and then looked at Sheriff Ironwood steadily, eye-to-eye.

"Here, Sheriff, I want you to have this before we leave here. I don't want anything to happen to it."

The sheriff took the small piece of sculptured stone, and then he turned to Father Juan.

"Father, would you go with us to find Andrew? I'm not sure why, but I sense it might be a good idea."

Father Juan took a couple of steps back into the office and nodded toward Sheriff Ironwood.

"Of course, Sheriff, if you think I can be of help. Certainly, I'll come with you."

The sheriff took Simon Peter by the arm, and the three men made their way down the hall to the dispatcher's desk near the front entrance. The sheriff could see Deputy Stark sitting behind the wheel of the department's red Jeep with the large Custer County Sheriff's Department badge on the door. The sheriff turned to Deputy Bebe.

"We're taking the suspect with us. Call the Highway Patrol's office and tell them we may need some assistance shortly. Tell their dispatcher that if Patrolman Gary Wolfe is on duty to send him to the Washita Battlefield site. And, get in touch with the sheriff in Roger Mills County. Tell him I'm crossing into his jurisdiction, and I would like to see him there as well. Got that?"

"Will do, Sheriff. Oh, Sheriff! Just got another call from that Joseph Humboldt fellow. He says to tell you he's got some info for you about the feathers."

"Okay. Call him back and tell him I'll be in touch soon. I think I already know what he is going to tell me. But, tell him, I'll get back to him. Oh! And let the Ranger at the Washita Battleground know we're on our way. Tell her we will need to search the park."

Sheriff Ironwood nodded toward the waiting Jeep. "Okay, Simon Peter, let's go see if we can find your blood-brother. I'd like to give him this little owl in person."

✝

TO KILL A MAN TWICE

Damn the spirit to hell

LEX SAT as still as he could. His butt was sore as hell, but he dared not move. The two sinister black holes, staring at him like the malevolent eyes of a deadly snake, made sure of that. The man who had secured him to the park bench sat across the concrete tabletop and was as still as his captive. The stranger had remained like that for over an hour, and Alex had given up trying to get him to talk, to explain what he wanted; to answer why he had kidnapped the performer in the first place.

Alex Austenne could see just off to his right that the morning light was beginning to show all along the high ridge that rose sharply from the river channel. As the early glow made the details of the elevation come to life, the Custer reenactor stared down at his boots, and suddenly it came to him, he thought he knew what was happening. He couldn't help himself; he smiled slightly as he again looked at the hills not far away.

He tried once more to get a response. "That's the Washita River, isn't it?" Alex paused. "And that's the ridge from which George Armstrong Custer and the Seventh Cavalry charged into the sleeping camp of the peace chief Black Kettle, isn't it?"

The light of the new day also brought into focus the face of his captor clearly. Alex recognized the dark skin features.

"You know, I suspected it would be you. I told my wife about your outburst at the reading. In a way, I've been expecting someone like you for a long time; we both have." Alex surprisingly felt a sense of relief. At least he knew who he was dealing with even though he didn't know his name or anything else about him.

"You a Cheyenne?" Alex didn't wait for an answer. "Of course you're a Cheyenne. Why else would we be here? If this is a joke, it's not very funny. Mister, you're going to be in one hell of a mess with this stunt. You know that don't you?"

Alex waited for a response, but none came. "Did some of the guys put you up to this…this joke? If they did, it's time we have a good laugh and bring this charade to a close. Don't you think?"

The man raised his gaze slightly and Alex could see his dark eyes, they stared at him without expression; stared at him like the double-barrel shotgun that was tied to a stand and pointed in Alex's direction. A string attached to the triggers connected the captive to the threat.

At last the stranger spoke. "*General Custer*, I am glad you know where you are. It's been a long time, but I suppose there are some things you never forget. Isn't that right?"

Alex didn't immediately know how to respond.

"I mean, it was here that you claimed what you described as your greatest victory. Isn't that so, *General*?"

Alex hesitated a moment more, but then decided to take the bait.

"Well, I suppose that's right," he said with what he knew must be a weak response. "My Seventh Cavalry did succeed in scattering some of the marauding Indians clear out into the Staked Plains of Texas. The good folks of Kansas, isolated as they were on their remote farms and ranches out on the prairie, could feel a bit safer in their beds at night after that battle; that they could."

Alex quickly felt his return to character. He waited for the reaction to the little barb he had flung at his captor. None came, and the *General* just as quickly reverted to Alex Austenne.

"Hey man," he blurted out. "I don't know what game you want to play here, but how about taking these damn cuffs off; my hands are numb; they're going to fall off if you don't release the pressure soon. Come on, what do you say?"

The man stood and slid his legs over the bench seat. Without comment, he slowly walked around the table and stopped directly behind Alex. Alex felt one of the cuffs release, and heard the rattle of the short chain. The man snapped the free cuff to a rail on the table where the two sat, and returned to his seat.

"Now, let me make something clear to you. I want to talk to the *General*, and only to him. Do you understand?"

Alex stared at the man for a long moment before he answered. "Not really," he answered and squirmed in his seat trying to encourage circulation in his backside.

"But I can play that part, and I can play it well. So I guess we can try that out...but, who are you? And, what's the endgame to this little pretense?"

"*General*, you say your white farmers felt safer in their beds after you slaughtered the village of my people and scattered them like so many quail out onto the prairie. How do you think that the mothers and fathers among those settlers felt about buying their safety with the blood of the mothers and children of Black Kettle's lodges on that winters morning in November? Do you suppose they thought of that massacre as justice? Or do you think they saw the scalps taken by the soldiers and their Osage scouts along the Washita as sweet revenge for what a few desperate Indians, a few Dog Soldiers, had done to some settlers trying to save their way of life? Do you think any of them even cared about such things? Cared about anything but themselves? Do you think that in times like these people think of the *others* as even human; as people with feelings like themselves?"

Alex stared at his kidnapper in disbelief. "Oh, oh, oh! I get it. I see this. I remember what you shouted in the Hall. *Murderer! Murderer!* you said. That's what this is about, isn't it? You want to argue about whether what happened on the Washita was a battle for justice or a massacre for revenge. Isn't that right?"

Alex turned his head and looked toward the river that was clearly visible now, illuminated by the morning bright sun. He had raised himself off the seat, but then his eyes reflexively focused on the shotgun staring back, and he gradually sat down.

"Yeah, I got it. You're the one that sent that package, too. The one who sent that feather dipped in blood aren't you? You're that spirit...that spirit of the Blood Feather thing;

aren't you?"

The dark eyes that stared at Alex as he spoke never wavered, but stayed fixed. Alex stared back for a moment.

"I want to talk with the *General,* and no one else. Do you understand me?"

"Yeah," Alex said reluctantly. "I understand you. I understand you perfectly," he responded. "What do you want, *Blood Feather*?" The *General* straightened up and stared intently at his adversary. He hoped the buttons on his military tunic were lined up properly.

✝

WAR DOESN'T REQUIRE AN ADJECTIVE

The residue

"WHAT WOULD YOU CALL it, *General Custer*; the actions of the Seventh Cavalry on the Washita River that cruelly cold November morning...would you describe what your troopers did a massacre or a battle? Was the murdering of women and children, and old men an act of revenge, or was it simply justice? What say you, *General*? It's the only question I have for you this day. This is why you are here."

The only sounds that broke through the silence that followed the man's question were the calls of the birds announcing their excitement at the new day, and the placid noise in the background of the river flowing lazily a short distance from two men sitting at the park bench table.

"It was neither," finally, was the *General's* response. "It was simply war." Alex looked up from the table and stared at his captor. "And war doesn't require an adjective, only an outcome. There is only one important duty in war, and that duty is to win it. In war you're either a winner or you're a loser. There's no second place prize."

Blood Feather leaned forward slowly and rested his elbows on the hard, cold rough surface of the concrete tabletop. He returned the stare.

"So then, *General*, the old saying that *all is fair in love and war* is more than just a funny quote. Is that it? Winning is all… destroying your enemy, destroying him even if it means destroying his way of life along with the victory. That's it? That's what the killing of Black Kettle, the killing of his squaws and their little ones, the killing of the Chief's entire herd of horses, the burning of his lodges, the destruction of his winter food stuffs, the elimination of the means of survival in the long prairie winter; this is what that attack in 1868, was about? You say then that it never was a question of revenge or justice, massacre or battle; only a question of winning the war. That's it?"

"That's what an army in war does. That's what the grand Northern Armies of General Grant and Sherman did only a few years before all throughout the rebellious South of General Lee. They shelled cities, burned crops, destroyed railway lines, shot civilians, robbed banks and food stores, herded shopkeepers and mothers out of their stores and homes and put them to flight until there was no more resistance to their force of arms; until there was no more plantation culture, until there was no more Negro slavery, until they had *destroyed a way of life*.

"Then the armies moved West, out onto the prairies and Great Plains, and began again. This time these armies were to make way for the expansion of the white man's culture; to spread it from sea to sea. To see that it fulfilled its *destiny*. Any resistance was deemed an act of war, and war, once begun, had to be won. You see, the notions of a just war are for the politicians and the philosophers; for the soldier, the ones doing the battle, these notions were irrelevant. For the soldier the idea that you would risk all to break a people's will, and then let all remain as it were is not only wrong-headed, but perverse. What I suspect you have failed to grasp, *Blood Feather*, is that the Seventh Cavalry was not on the Washita River to arrest wrongdoers, we weren't there to punish the many for what a few Indian Dog Soldiers had done. We were there on that ugly November morning to destroy. And destroy is what we did. And, if it's not too much for you to understand, we did a damn good job of it."

Blood Feather straightened his back and offered a quiet smile for a long moment.

"No, *General Custer*, that's where you're wrong; where your spirit has always been wrong. I understand very well why you led your Seventh Cavalry to do what you did to my people. I've never been under any illusion otherwise."

Blood Feather paused long enough to retrieve a small canvas bag that had been resting at his feet. As he laid it on his lap, he unzipped the bag, and the *General* watched as the man removed two medical syringes. He laid both on the table. Then the Indian took two vials from the bag. They looked to contain a liquid that filled three-quarters of the vials. Last, he arranged an elastic cord between the vials and the syringes.

"*General*, I'm going to tell you what you have been asking all along. What am I doing? What do I want from you?"

As he spoke he picked up one of the syringes and

removed the bright yellow plastic that protected the needle point. He then carefully inserted the needle into one of the vials and pulled the liquid into the syringe until it was nearly full. *Blood Feather* tapped the syringe and squirted a few drops into the air.

"I've brought you here for a test of your spirit. We will finally get to the spirit of the *General*. Finally bring him out into the open and see his nature. Finally deal with an ancient wrong done to my people."

Blood Feather wrapped the elastic cord around his upper left arm and waited for the veins to protrude abnormally. He then pushed the needle through the skin and slowly transferred the liquid into the vein.

"What the hell are you doing? Man, are you crazy? What's that? What the hell?"

Alex Austenne came back to the moment. The *General* had evaporated into the morning air just as the mist had burned off with the heat of the sun. He began to nervously look one way and the then the next, for what he had no idea. Where in the holy-hell are the people, the rangers that run this fuckin' place? he thought.

"I've just given *Blood Feather's* spirit an overdose of heroin, *General Custer*."

Alex started instinctively to stand, but then he stopped as he again glanced at the shotgun. He settled back into his seat.

"You did what? For Christ's sake man, enough is enough. This stupid game is over. I'm not Custer and you're not some ancient Indian spirit. Now turn me loose and get that frigin' shotgun out of my face."

The Indian returned the empty syringe to its position next

to the second one. As he did he reached into his shirt pocket and retrieved something. Alex watched him intently as he pitched a small key across the table to Alex.

"Here, release yourself," he said quietly without emotion. In a few minutes, I am going to become very drowsy and then I will pass out most likely. In a few minutes after that, I will be dead. I will have killed my body, and I will have killed my spirit. You are the only one that can save me, *General.*"

Alex just stared at his captor for a second. "Man you are a whacko of the first order."

The man ignored Alex's taunt. "I will die, that is unless you inject me with this," he said as he held up the second syringe.

"This is the antidote. You can save this Indian or you can let him die. It is your choice. Either way you will be free to go. I'm betting that you will do what you have always done, *General*; you will let the Indian perish when you had the chance to save him. You will kill his body and you will kill his spirit. You will kill him twice. He will be gone for all time."

Blood Feather reached out and pushed the second syringe a few inches closer to Alex.

Alex could only stare at it.

"It will be your choice just as it was before when you and your soldiers took the spirit of Black Kettle and flung it into the waters of the Washita."

"Okay, okay! I've got it. But...but what about this damn gun you've got pointed at me? What about that?"

Blood Feather smiled slightly. "It's not loaded, *General*," he said. "It never has been. Those hammers are cocked over empty chambers. Just release the cuff and unhook that trigger string, and you can walk away. Do it! You can do it right now; I'll be on my face in a few more minutes. You're free, *General*. Your spirit is free to roam; to continue your journey through time that never ends; through space unbounded. You don't have to worry about this Indian anymore. I've made my point."

"Point, what the hell point is that?"

Again the man smiled slightly.

"You're carrying the spirit of George Armstrong Custer," *Blood Feather* said with a slur. "He lives in you. The *General* rides you like he did his favorite horse. You have carried him for a very long time. You've let him run free among all those that so admire the man; all those that wish for the return of the great soldier: all those who would gladly ride by his side if they only could."

"Man are you one for the funny farm. Look! Look at me! I'm a frigin' actor. You hear me: an actor, nothing more. Your ancestors killed Custer, you hear me you dope-head? He's dead, dead, dead! Got it?"

Alex tried the key on the handcuff holding him. To his surprise it worked, so he gingerly removed the constraint. As he did, Alex detached the string running from it to the shotgun. He swung his legs over the bench and stood up, pausing long enough to stamp his feet into the ground several times to push the blood back into his legs. He looked at the Indian who was nodding his head and glanced at the gun and stepped clear of its line of sight. Alex wondered if the man had told him the truth so he reached down and grabbed the triggering string and jerked it hard. Both hammers slammed home simultaneously. Two loud clicks sounded, not even loud enough to stop the birds from singing.

"I don't get it. But, I can tell you this, Chief, if Custer's spirit is working in me right now, then I'm going to do now what he did all those years ago right here on this river. I'm going to make a strategic retreat. You hear me? Man, do you hear me? I'm out of here. If you die from a drug overdose, you've done it to yourself. You're on your own nickel my red friend. *On your own!*" Alex turned and took a step.

"My name is Andrew Straw," the man said in a whisper and lowered his head onto his outstretched arm on the hard tabletop.

Alex Austenne turned his head and looked over his shoulder at the figure. He stared at the man, who now had a name, for a long moment.

"Well, Mr. Straw, the *General* is about to leave the building. Adios, Chief!"

Alex walked the few steps to the gravel trail and started to backtrack up the hill. He made about ten paces and stopped and looked back again at the table. He stood still for a few moments watching to see if the man moved. He didn't. He had cradled his head in his arms, and all Alex could see was the top of his head. He took a few more steps before he stopped again, and then turned.

"Dammit to hell," he said as he exhaled forcefully. Alex retraced his steps back to the table and stood still for a long while watching the man that lay as still as a corpse. His eyes fell on the second syringe. Alex had never given a shot in his life. He'd seen it done in the movies, but that was it. He picked it up and looked at the pink liquid that filled about three-quarters of the tube.

"This is crazy," Alex said under his breath. The man lay as still as a stone, and Alex could see that his hands had spread open, his fingers lying limp on the table. He again looked up the trail, instinctively thinking about going for help, but then he looked back at the man. He didn't appear to be breathing. Alex put his ear close to his head, but all he heard was a slight gurgling sound; like phlegm rattling in his throat.

Alex let out a long sigh. "Okay, okay! What the hell I'm doing this for, I have no idea." He reached for and grabbed Andrew's wrist, and pulled his arm out from under his head. The man's skull thudded against the hard tabletop as Alex twisted his arm to expose the underside of his forearm. One large vein made itself available, and Alex pushed the plunger slightly to do what he always saw them do with a syringe. A few drops squirted out and ran down the syringe and onto Alex's hand.

"Okay, *Blood Feather*, here goes nothing." To Alex's surprise the needle punctured the vein efficiently, and he pushed the liquid into it without hesitation.

Now what? He thought. He scrutinized Andrew Straw closely for a moment, but there was no sign of any change. Alex could see the unconscious man's pulse still pushing blood through his wrist so he knew he was still alive.

"Why did I do that?" he said softly to himself. "Shit man! What did you get me to do?"

Again Alex scanned up the trail for any signs of other people in the area. The only sounds he heard were some distant quail doing call and response; nothing else. He wondered why this place was so deserted. For a national park, it was a lonely place he thought.

"To hell with it," he said to the lifeless bulk lying still and showing no signs of reviving. Alex put the syringe down on the table and headed back to the trail. He took one final glance back at the man who said he was Andrew Straw before he moved at a deliberate pace up the slope. In only a few moments, Alex had left behind the last several hours of what he wasn't sure. He reached in his coat pocket to feel for his keys. They were still there, so he quickened his pace again. There was only one thing to do now, and that was to find some help for the Indian lying face down on that park tabletop.

Alex broke into a quickstep pace, and then into a jog. He topped a low ridge, and the trail broke sharply to the left. That's when he spotted a figure in the morning light headed right for him. Alex waved his arms and shouted.

"Judging by your outfit, you must be Alex Austenne," deputy Raaven Stark said. "We've been looking for you."

Alex bent over slightly to catch his breath.

"Well, you've found me," he muttered; then he turned and pointed back down the trail to the river. "There's a crazy guy close to the river. He's lying on a park bench. I think he took a drug overdose. He's the one who took me. I tried to save…"

"Whoa, Mr. Austenne. Easy!" Deputy Stark pressed the call button on her shoulder. "I've got him, Sheriff. He's okay. We're only about a quarter-mile from you. Just take the main trail. We'll wait right here. The suspect who did this is nearby; we'll wait."

"This guy is a nutcase," Alex stammered.

"Okay, we'll sort this out shortly. Are you okay? He didn't hurt you did he?"

"No, no, nothing like that. I'm okay."

"All right. I'm Deputy Stark of the Custer County Sheriff's Office. Sheriff Ironwood will be here shortly, and we'll try to find out what this is all about."

"Good luck!" Alex said mostly to himself as he looked directly at Raaven Stark. "Deputy, you'd better hurry. I think the guy's in bad shape."

"Okay, Mr. Austenne; we will; we will."

✝

STANDING IN THE DUST

Waiting for Grace

IRONWOOD LEANED AGAINST THE OKLAHOMA HIGHWAY PATROL CRUISER as he watched the flashing blue, red and yellow lights of the Custer County Regional EMS ambulance top the hill and quickly disappear. The sound of the sirens slowly faded and then grew silent. The old lawman was tired; tired to the bone as they say.

Sheriff Nathan Crocker and Patrolman Gary Wolfe were approaching so he straightened up and walked a few steps to meet the other lawmen.

"Seth, now that the dust has settled, you want to fill me in on what that was all about?" Sheriff Crocker asked. "I damn sure don't mind you coming to Roger Mills County to help me out, Lord knows I need it, but I suspect I better know why. You understand, reports, and all that dad-burn paperwork stuff." Nate Crocker flashed a big grin toward Seth. The ancient sheriff was famous for that grin. It was mostly because one of his front teeth was missing, and when he grinned it looked like you could see all the way to the interior of his vastly oversized stomach through the dark portal.

Sheriff Ironwood shot a glance toward Gary Wolfe and nodded his greeting; the patrolman did likewise.

"Nate, if I knew I'd tell you, but I'm mostly in the dark on this one myself."

Sheriff Nate looked over at the Custer County Sheriff's emblem on the side of the white Jeep Cherokee. "Would it have something to do with that young man in the back seat?"

Seth Ironwood shook his head yes. "It has everything to do with him, Nate. I just don't have all the pieces of the puzzle put together yet. That man's name is Simon Peter Straw, and the one they hauled out of here is, at least I hope he still is, his brother, Andrew Straw."

"Twins?"

"Yeah, identical. These two had made some kind of oath...hold on, Nate. How about you give me a ride back to Custer County, and I'll try to explain what I know about what just happened here."

"Sure, Seth. You've surely got this sheriff's sniffer turned to the air."

"Okay, then. Give me a sec. I need to talk to my deputy for a minute."

Sheriff Ironwood looked at the Highway Patrolman. "Gary, would you mind giving Mr. Austenne a ride back to my jail? I want to get his statement as soon as I get back."

"Can do that, Seth."

"Oh, and Gary; if he is so inclined, let him talk about what happened here. It might be helpful to compare notes down the line."

"Can do that too."

"Thanks, Gary…lunch is on me next time."

"Be right back, Nate."

Ironwood moved quickly toward the sheriff's car, as Deputy Stark came to meet him.

"Raaven, take Simon Peter home. I'm going to ride back with Sheriff Crocker, and Patrolman Wolfe will take Alex Austenne with him."

Deputy Stark looked over her shoulder towards the Jeep. "Do you want me to talk to Simon on the way back about his brother's condition?"

"No, leave it for now. We don't know much anyway. I'll see what I can find out over the radio on the way back."

Ironwood turned to leave, but then abruptly wheeled back around. "Raaven, I almost forgot…where's Father Juan? I haven't seen him since we got here."

The deputy glanced at the sheriff with a bit of a quizzical look. "I thought you knew, Sheriff. The Father got into the ambulance with Andrew Straw. He said he might be needed given the boy's condition."

The sheriff looked away for a second. "Yeah, I see. I should have known he would. Okay then, on your way…I'll meet you back at the jail."

"I'm ready if you are, Nate; let's get going."

ಬ

"Well?" Sheriff Nate looked with a quick glance toward Seth Ironwood sitting stoically in the passenger's seat.

"Well, what?" was his response.

"Seth, are you going to tell me what's going on with this case, or not?" Sheriff Nate abruptly turned east on Highway 47 and made the sharp curve past the imposing stone structure that was the Washita Battlefield National Museum and Visitor Center.

"Nate, I'm just trying to find a place to start this story. It's hard to explain something you don't understand yourself." Seth turned to stare out the window of the sheriff's cruiser at the stretch of scrub oak that dotted the landscape on his side of the highway. As usual there were a few cattle roaming the depleted pasture searching for anything green, anything edible.

Sheriff Nate headed back east toward Cheyenne, Oklahoma. "Okay, Seth, why don't you just tell me what you know. Let's start with these two brothers; these twins. What about them?"

Again Seth stared out the passenger window for a moment before he spoke. "That's easy; we know everything about their physical world, but next to nothing about anything else except what Simon Peter Straw has told us. Twin brothers, Native American heritage, likely abused as youth by a violent, alcoholic stepfather, impoverished upbringing...the one bright spot in their youth was the education they received at a Catholic school in South Dakota.

"The one brother, Andrew, went into the army and became an Army Ranger; served a tour in Afghanistan. According to his record, he was sent home due to a combat injury...not physical but psychological. He suffered from PTSD; not sure how severe, but enough that the army recommended some form of therapy and counseling.

"The other brother, Simon Peter, is a bit vaguer…attended college, as far as we could tell several of them. He did have a degree in anthropology. But, other than that, we don't know a whole lot about him before he turned up on our doorstep claiming to be a killer."

Sheriff Ironwood paused as Nate slowed to pass through the junction of Highways 33 and 34 and into the little town of Hammon. Seth always had the same thought about these western Oklahoma one-horse towns—why? He looked at the mostly empty ancient store fronts during the short minute it took to clear the town.

"Was he?" Sheriff Nate interrupted Seth's thoughts.

Seth turned to the driver, "No. It was all an elaborate fantasy of imagined justice or revenge or whatever, cooked up by the two brothers years before. Just a fantasy to settle an ancient wrong; a wrong the boys felt strongly needed righting—a wrong that happened at the very place where Andrew Straw was taken on a stretcher and loaded into that ambulance."

Sheriff Nate returned the cruiser to highway speed as they left Hammon.

"Some fantasy, Seth. Sounds like it got a lot more serious than that. You think?"

"Yeah, I think. Why don't you call the hospital, Nate, let's check on the status of Andrew."

"Will do." The old sheriff took note of the sign that told him the city limits of Butler was five miles ahead as he depressed the button on his shoulder microphone.

8

The silence was awkward as the two lawmen rode along Highway 33, heading east. Finally, Sheriff Nathaniel Crocker ventured a word.

"You know, Seth, I've been in this business for a lot of years, maybe too many, but I never get used to news like that. I never get used to the senseless nature of it. How is a young man like that, a man with his whole life still to come, is all of a sudden dead? And what's more puzzling is that the reason is all about some crazy notion of justice, or something like that. How is it, Seth?"

Sheriff Nate waited for a response, but the silence prevailed. He glanced at his friend.

"Seth, you okay?"

Finally, the lawman answered his comrade. "No...I don't think so, Nate." Seth Ironwood straightened in his seat, and shifted slightly towards the driver.

"Nate, I know you will think I've fallen off the edge, but something just snapped when you said Andrew Straw had died. I mean, I felt it. And it hurt."

Sheriff Nate noted the Arapaho city limits marker, "You kind of got caught up with those lads, didn't you, Seth?"

"Yeah, I suppose I did. And that's what is difficult about all this. I don't know why. I mean this was just another case to solve—crazy maybe, but still another one like the thousands I have seen over my career. So why these two? For Christ sake, I didn't even know Andrew Straw—had never even met him."

The sheriff's cruiser crossed Highway 183 and slowed down as it approached North 7th. The driver turned south from Arapaho Road onto 7th as Seth Ironwood looked first at the few scattered trailer homes skirted and made permanent in the neighborhood. Then he turned his gaze toward the familiar façade of the Custer County Jail Facility. It was relatively new, and its institutional starkness gave it the look of foreboding that Sheriff Ironwood both hated and knew was necessary. The two men looked at each other as Sheriff Nate navigated into the side entrance.

"You going to charge Simon Peter?" he said as he killed the engine.

"With what, Nate?"

"Seth, you know as well as I. There's at least a half-a-dozen charges that would stick; how about obstruction of justice to start?"

Seth looked straight ahead for a moment.

"Yeah, you're right. That's a place to start. And, of course, then there is making a false confession; conspiracy to commit kidnapping; and certainly we could make a good case for accessory to murder/suicide. The State of Oklahoma has cause to house this young man for most of any productive years he will ever have. And, on top of it all, Simon Peter has to bury his twin brother. Let's get the big stone wheel of justice a rolling, what do you say, Sheriff?"

Nate Crocker stared at his colleague for a very long moment. He couldn't comprehend what was happening with his long-time friend.

"Seth, like I said, you're a little too close to this one. Maybe this one is for Deputy Stark; what do you think?"

"I'm sorry, Nate. I'm not thinking straight. It's just it seems more than ironic to me that these boys came searching for justice for what they saw as an ancient wrong, but now one is dead and the other faces the full wrath of the law. And, at the end of the day, all we can do is hide and watch.

Where's the sense in that? Where's the justice?"

Before Sheriff Nate could answer, Seth put his hand on the door handle, "Guess I better get in there and get back to work. I need to see what Austenne has to say about of all this. Thanks for the lift. I'll send the whole report to you as soon as I get it sorted out. I appreciate your patience, and your ear."

"Hey! What are old worn-out sheriffs good for anyway? You'd do the same for me in a heartbeat. Your badge is always welcomed in Roger Mills County, Seth."

Sheriff Ironwood exited the cruiser, but paused to lean back in. "Yes, I would, Nate."

†

THE LAST, LAST STAND

King's X

A LEX AUSTENNE LOOKED ANXIOUSLY AT SHERIFF IRONWOOD as the tall lanky man entered the small room where the Custer reenactor had waited for over an hour. The sheriff sat down opposite and rested his elbows on the metal tabletop. He dreaded saying what he was about to say. Before he could begin, Alex stood up nervously.

"How is that guy doing? Is he okay? I mean he really looked to be in bad shape when they put him on the stretcher. Is he okay?"

"Mr. Austenne, please. Sit down. The news is not good."

"Not good, what do you mean? I gave him the antidote; you know like he said to do. Not good; how is that? I did...I did what he told me. You know that, don't you, Sheriff?"

"Andrew Straw died before they made it to the hospital. He opened his eyes one time according to Father Juan, and then he passed away."

Alex sat and stared back at the sheriff. The news was of the type that its rawness would not quickly process as a rational declaration; it was of the type that needed more sorting, and enhancement by recollection before the mind could accept it.

"Mr. Austenne, I need you to tell me exactly what happened from the very beginning until you met the deputy on that trail. Can you do that?"

"I didn't kill that man, Sheriff."

"From the beginning, Mr. Austenne."

Alex appeared to slump a bit in his chair before he began. "I guess you would say it started the night before at my performance. That man…"

"Andrew Straw, Mr. Austenne, his name was Andrew Straw."

"Well, yes. Mr. Straw stood up in the middle of one of my monologues and shouted at the stage—I think it was *murderer, murderer,* or something to that effect. Well that stopped the show in its tracks. That is until he abruptly turned and left the hall. But, as they say, the show must go on, so I collected myself and continued."

"And, then, what happened?"

"Well, nothing actually; that is, until after the performance. That's when he kidnapped me in the parking lot, and the next thing I know we are walking down this trail in the dark…Sheriff, do you think I killed him; killed Andrew Straw?"

ॐ

Sheriff Ironwood stood up and turned towards the heavy metal portal to the interview room. He walked slowly to the door and grasped the handle as he thought about all he had heard. The sheriff hadn't been expecting Mr. Austenne's admission that he had injected Andrew Straw with some substance from a second syringe. That just didn't compute.

Alex Austenne asked again with a tone that was just short of frantic, "You don't think I killed him, do you, Sheriff?"

Sheriff Ironwood delayed his response for effect. "No...but he killed something in you," he added with an absence of emotion in his voice.

"What?...What do you mean by that?"

"I don't know what I mean, Mr. Austenne. I wish I did."

The sheriff turned back to Mr. Austenne. "Have you been able to speak to your wife sense you arrived here?"

"No, Sheriff. They brought me straight to this room and instructed me to wait for your arrival."

"Well, come with me. We'll make that happen."

Alex stood up slowly. "Does that mean, I'm free to go?"

The sheriff smiled slightly, "Of course, unless you have something else to tell me—do you?"

"No, Sheriff, I don't. But, I would like to ask you a question."

"What's that?"

"What killed Andrew Straw, Sheriff?"

Sheriff Seth Ironwood looked past Alex Austenne, the famous Custer reenactor, and down the long corridor which led to the front offices of the Custer County Jail.

As he took the first step towards them, he spoke. "General George Armstrong Custer killed him, Mr. Austenne. The *General* killed him."

✝

BUTTERFINGERS IN A HOT CAR

Sticky fingers taste good

S IT POSSIBLE, SHERIFF, AFTER ALL THAT HAS HAPPENED, to see your jail facilities?" Father Juan looked a bit apprehensive as he sat down across from Seth Ironwood's desk. It had been nearly a month since Andrew Straw had died. The young man had died as Father Juan had held his hand, and as the priest administered the Sacrament of Last Rites amid the blaring sirens spewing out a cacophony of noise that scattered all in their path.

The sheriff looked at his guest quizzically for a second before he answered the father's request.

"Sure, Father, I'd be happy to show you around. I'm just a bit puzzled why you want to see our little hotel. It's rather a stark place. We've tried to hire a concierge, but the county is having none of that; tight budgets, and all of that, you see." The sheriff raised his eyebrows to give accent to his ill-conceived attempt at humor; a joke that the sheriff regretted even before the words had faded into silence.

To the sheriff the impression that the priest seemed to have missed the joke was a relief.

"I suppose you could say, Sheriff, that it's sort of in our job description to go to the downtrodden in such stark places that they are most often found. And after Andrew, I feel a priestly need to think more about what happens to people that find themselves caught up in our criminal justice system. You see, I have to make a priestly confession of my own; I have been less than attentive to these people."

"Yeah, I got you. Come on then let's take the tour; although, I must warn you that there is really not much to see—a lot of hard bars, concrete, and overly thin mattresses. And as for criminals, right now the most dangerous desperado we have got caught stealing candy bars at the Piggly-Wiggly. It seems he couldn't afford the Butterfingers, but he couldn't resist the urge. It was kind of a mess, and I mean that literally. The poor fellow had fifteen of the chocolate logs stuffed in his underwear. The jailer said he was the strangest strip search he had ever seen. He said the prisoner kept wiping his privates and licking his fingers. Pardon me Father, for the crudeness; but how gross is that?"

The two men smiled at each other as they approached the heavy steel door with one small double-thick glass near the top-center of the frame. The sheriff pushed a button, and the door lock made a clunking echo down the long corridor as it released its grip. He removed his Kimber .45 from the quick-release holster at his hip and pushed the gunmetal gray weapon into a small steel locker next to the jail entrance and turned the key to set the lock.

"After you, Father," he said and quickly stepped into the room of cells and closed the door behind him. The lock again echoed as it found its home. Father Juan and Sheriff Ironwood were the only ones in the room who could walk down the line of seven cells. The houseguests were confined to the first two small five-by-seven rectangle heavy-barred enclosures that displayed only two primitive bunks next to the wall, stacked one upon the other, and a single no-lid toilet in the far corner.

The sheriff nodded toward the occupant of the first cell as they walked slowly down the hall.

"That's the Butterfinger Kid in number one," he said softly. The man in the cell was asleep and paid no apparent attention to the visitors as they passed. Father Juan couldn't get the image of a naked man covered in black chocolate as he looked at the figure curled up tightly on the bottom bunk. Some things of the real world were simply beyond the priest's scope.

The occupant of cell number two was standing against the bars as they approached. He appeared to be hungering for some company. The sheriff paused in front of the prisoner who was clothed in the county orange jumpsuit.

"Father, I want you to meet our most loyal tenant. This here is none other than Mr. Timothy Turnipp."

The inmate smiled widely at the sheriff, displaying a toothless, but not unattractive smile. He was a small, wiry type not more than five feet tall. His countenance was partially hidden by a thick salt-and-pepper beard that overpowered his face, and his eyes were deep brown and as bright as the overheard naked light on the ceiling just over his right shoulder.

"Tim, meet Father Juan Bosco. He's the parish priest at St. Mary's." The prisoner recreated his toothless grin to the priest in acknowledgment but didn't speak.

Father Juan directed is question to the sheriff. "Turnipp? Is that his real name?" the father said as he tried unsuccessfully to repress a smile.

"For sure it is. Mr. Turnipp comes to us usually on average about once a week. You see, Timothy here has a bit of a problem with the bottle. But I have a theory about that. I don't think it's so much with the booze as it is that Tim doesn't like to work on the outside; he'd rather panhandle. But the problem with that is he only gets enough from that occupation to satisfy his need for drink. It doesn't leave anything for meals, you see. Isn't that right, Tim?" The sheriff didn't wait for a response because he knew there wouldn't be one.

"So, the solution for this toothless wonder is to make himself obnoxious enough to the locals so he will be eligible for accommodations in our fine facilities. Which, as you might expect, comes with meals and fresh linens. Now, you should also understand that our friend here is most willing to earn his keep. He's one of the most particular janitors I have ever known. Tim is the reason this place stays so tidy all the time. Isn't that right my bearded friend?"

Again the inmate merely flashed his signature grin, but not a word of acknowledgment of the sheriff's praise.

As the sheriff and Father Juan took a step to move to the next cell, Mr. Turnipp stuck his arm out through the bars and lightly touched the priest. The father stopped and turned to face the man.

"Yes, Timothy; do you want to say something to me?"

The question was only met with another broad smile.

"He doesn't talk, Father," the sheriff interrupted. "I've never heard him say a word, and he's been with us for a couple of years; like I said, on-and-off."

Father Juan smiled back and made the sign of the cross in Timothy's direction. "Bless you Mr. Turnipp," he said. Tim withdrew his arm through the bars and hesitantly signed the cross himself. He then put his palms together as if in prayer and offered a slight bow to the priest. As the strange inmate did so, he opened his hands and turned them up. Father Juan realized that this man had taken the Eucharist before. He suspected the man was a Catholic, but before he could ask him the question the sheriff touched his elbow.

"Come on, Father, I'll show you our special accommodation. It's at the end of this row.

As the two men moved along the row of cells, Father Juan noticed the small numbers above the heavy doors. All the cells offered no privacy from those adjacent to them until they reached cell number seven.

"As you can see, this last cell; cell seven, has a solid wall on either side. The deputies call it the *bridal suite*. A bit more private than the others." Sheriff Ironwood opened the heavy barred door and stepped into the seventh cell. You want to join me?"

The priest surveyed the opening for a second and then moved tentatively into the enclosure. "You won't shut that door will you, Sheriff?" he said as he presented a feeble smile.

"Here is where we keep our really hard cases; and, I'm afraid you wouldn't qualify, so don't worry. We've had some pretty bad actors in this small space, I can tell you that.

These solid walls on both sides keep the prisoner in cell seven isolated visually from the run-of-the-mill types we normally have in our jail."

Father Juan looked around, and then he sat down on the bottom bunk. He pushed his fingers into the mattress covered with a single grey wool blanket. "Not too bad. A little small for my taste, but it's got a nice firmness to it. Not too bad at all."

"I can arrange for you to spend a night or two if you'd like."

"No, no, no. That's okay, Seth. I've got my spot already. Thanks anyway. I'm curious though. Who was the worst guy you've had to sleep on this bed?"

The sheriff crossed the narrow cell and leaned his back against the far cinder block wall.

"Actually, the hardest case we've had in this cell was a woman. Oh, I've had some pretty bad guys in here too; but this one was one for the books, as they say."

Father Juan stood up and put his right arm on the top bunk leaning against it for support.

"And to look at her you wouldn't believe she was capable of what she did," Sheriff Ironwood continued. "She was quite pretty; short and shapely as I remember. Her blond hair was as rich as gold in the sun, and her quick smile would stun you in the same way. She was the closest thing to an angel I'd ever seen."

The sheriff paused and walked to the front of the cell, then turned back to face the priest.

"Okay, Sheriff. You've aroused my curiosity. What did she do?"

"She killed her mother," the sheriff again paused. "Oh, it wasn't the murder that was unusual, but the way she went about it. You see, the mother had severe Alzheimer's; practically a vegetable. The daughter, her name was Sally, had cared for her for several years. Sally always took her mother with her when she went shopping. We'd see them all the time around our little town. The mother, if I remember correctly, her name was Francine, never left the car. She always sat in the back seat on the opposite side to the driver.

"One hot summer day in August we found Francine sitting in the car in the parking lot of that strip mall just on the edge of the commercial district. Some store clerk found her and called 911. The windows were all rolled up. The coroner said the temperature inside the car was something like 175 degrees. The old woman was just sitting in the back seat; her eyes were still open and she looked as normal as I do now, but she was as dead as the engine of that car."

"Excuse me, Sheriff; kind of sounds like a terrible accident. No?"

"Oh yeah. We thought the same thing at first. A stupid mistake, and you don't normally consider murder in the shadow of stupidity. Sally told us that she had left the windows cracked, and the motor running when she went to do her shopping. That made sense because that's what she did all the time. She claimed that her mother somehow must have closed the windows; they were the powered kind. And then, what she told us was that she had left the air-conditioner set to high. Like I said, stupid, but not criminal.

"Sally was really beside herself. If anything, we all felt sorry for her. You know that's a terrible thing to go through;

seeing your mother roasted like a turkey. But then things began to get a little strange.

"Our coroner, his name is Bob Pesca, told me he wasn't sure why, but he wanted to impound Sally's car for a couple of days. At that bit of news, Sally's expression of grief changed instantly to one of anger. She protested as Shakespeare said, *a bit too strongly*. It raised some suspicions that probably wouldn't have surfaced otherwise.

"Bob took the car to the county garage to look it over. One of the things he did was start it and leave to idle. Well, when he did it the first time the engine quit after about five minutes. He did it again. It quit again at about the same interval of time. Bob did it a total of ten times, and each time he got the same results. Now old Mr. Pesca had seen a lot of strange things in his many years as our coroner, so he decided to take the car to the Ford dealership and have them see what was wrong with it; why it quit running as it did."

Sheriff Ironwood interrupted his story and walked to the bunk and sat down. He was quiet for a moment until Father Juan said: "And?"

"And," the sheriff looked up and picked up the story, "the mechanics discovered a really strange glitch in the car's computer. It seems in the ignition program there was a piece of code that told the car to do exactly what it was doing. It shut off the engine.

"The problem was they couldn't explain why that was so; they'd never seen that particular malfunction before. A computer glitch, most of those who looked at it said. Well, if that had been all the evidence that pointed to foul play in Francine's death, we would have probably just scratched our heads and moved on. You know, my little department does not have any computer whizzes, and certainly no CSI type. I myself don't know a bit from a bite so to speak.

"But, then as they say *oh what a tangled web we weave when first we practice to deceive* came into play. You see, James Highsmith came to see me. Now Mr. Highsmith is our little community's insurance mogul. If you've got insurance around these parts, you probably bought it from him. He told me he just wanted to check with me about Sally's mother's death before he delivered the life insurance check. It seems that Sally had very recently taken out a $150,000 policy on her sweet mom. And the policy had cost her a bundle considering the condition of her mother. Well, that started a chain reaction. We got serious about the investigation. James put a hold on the settlement, and I sent off a request to the state to send a computer expert to investigate the code program in Sally's car.

"Well, to cut to the chase, everything began to unwind like a cat playing with a ball of string. It wasn't but a couple of weeks after that that our sweet, lovely Sally was balling like a baby in this very cell. The thing that sewed it up tight in a bundle turned out to be the computer glitch. Sweet Sally had paid a computer hacker, some guy out of Ireland; believe it or not, to mess with the car's code. When Sally heard that little piece of our evidence the rest was easy."

"What happened to her?"

"Well, you see the State of Oklahoma is a tad harsh with killers of that kind; those cold-blooded types. Sally was given the lethal cocktail about a year back. Those that witnessed her execution said it was like watching an angel die. They said she never squirmed, not one bit. She simply went to sleep. Father, I have often wondered that if Sally met up with Francine in the afterlife what the old mom might say to her sweet daughter. It would be a conversation worth hearing I betcha'. You think?"

"Yes I do. You know, a big part of my day is about trying to get folks to think about the reckoning to come before they do some of the things they do."

"Well, Father, if you think about it; we are sort of in the same profession. I swear, I do believe that a majority of people get out of bed in the morning and the first piece of clothing they put on is their stupid hat. At least that's the way it seems to be in Custer County."

Sheriff Ironwood let out a short sigh that drew Father Juan's notice. It didn't seem to be connected to the tale he had just heard.

He looked at the sheriff for a moment. "Seth, is there something else on your mind?"

The sheriff didn't answer directly; but only stared at the concrete floor between his boots.

"Yeah, I guess there is. I've had it on my mind ever since that day in the church; you know when we sent that white bird up as a messenger."

"You mean the white raven?"

"Yeah, the white raven."

"You want to go back to your office, Sheriff?

The sheriff stood up and extended his long frame in front of the bunk.

"No, not really. By some strange notion, this little cell seems to be the right place to tell you another story. Kind of reminds me of that spot in the church where you hear all those...those..."

"Confessions?"

"Yeah, all those confessions."

✝

Confessions in Cell Seven

The baggage handler in black

THERE WAS A MINOR commotion from down the row of cells so Sheriff Ironwood got up from the bunk and walked out into the hallway. No other noise followed the first so he returned to cell seven and walked to the back concrete wall and leaned his back against the cold blocks.

"Why don't you take my seat on the bunk, Father; I've got a story to tell you. It's the one I wanted to tell you at the church but couldn't get it to come out then."

Father Juan followed the sheriff's direction and sat down. He inclined slightly back and put his hands on the bunk behind him to support his frame. He didn't speak, which prompted the sheriff to begin.

Seth Ironwood reached into his pocket and retrieved the jade owl, and clutched it in his right hand.

"It starts a long time ago; actually about 1960. I was a very young and a gung-ho new second lieutenant in the Marines.

President Kennedy had sent my unit to Viet Nam. We were a special recon bunch; mostly intelligence gathering types. We had not been in country long when we were sent out from base camp up to the north; actually farther north than any other unit had been in the early days of that war. If I remember correctly it was our second day out and we were near a small hamlet identified on our maps as PouNap: a real nothing kind of place. There were only about twenty of us, and we had just moved out that morning and were crossing some rice paddies on some narrow walk bridges when we took hostile fire from somewhere near that village.

"Well as green as we were, we were still well trained, and, thank goodness that training took hold in a hurry. Luckily no one was hit, but we all were up to our necks in water. I remember that several of us rested our AR-15s on those land bridges and returned fire right into what we thought was the source of the hostile rounds. I remember I emptied two clips myself."

The sheriff shifted his weight against the wall from shoulder to shoulder before he continued.

"When we stopped sending our ordinance into the village we waited for a reaction. The unit must have sat in that muck for near a half-hour. There was no more fire incoming, and all we could hear sounded like moaning, but we weren't sure what it was. There were a bunch of dogs barking and howling too. I sent one of my sergeants forward to take a look. We watched him move among the small grass huts and disappear, all ready to fire if he got into trouble. Then he came back into sight and waved all of us forward.

"When we got into that hamlet it became apparent immediately what the effect of our return fire had been. I can still see that image to this day, Father. It's one you can never shed. All around the unit as it moved among the small dwelling lay the bodies of women and children; most of them dressed in those black pajamas we called them. There was blood and the worse kind of gore everywhere you looked. You have to understand how incredibly destructive our automatic rifles were when it came to destroying human tissue. The evidence of that horrific efficiency was scattered like butchered meat all around us. But what struck us most was the realization that among all the dead there wasn't one grown male, none; only women and children.

"A couple of my guys couldn't hold there breakfast and vomited. We all felt sick, I can tell you that. I instructed the sergeant to get a tally on the dead for our report. I had just finished that order and was turning around when the world for me went black. And, I mean it just like that: black. The next thing I was conscious of was waking up in a naval hospital state side. They told me at the time I had been shot in the neck in that village two months before and hadn't been conscious since. They said at the time I was shot nobody thought I would make it. A couple of times on the evac helicopter they told me I appeared to die, but each time I revived so they kept working on me.

"The point I am getting to, Father, is that for all that period I was dead to this world; for two months I was somewhere else. You might say, I was someone else. Then the dreams started.

"It was about five years later. At first they were very vague. Most of the time I couldn't remember them at all; they would fade away almost as soon as I got out of bed. But, after a while, fragments would stay with me; sometimes for a day or two. And then the dreams started taking on a very real structure, and more and more detail would stay with me during the day. And then they faded away again. I thought I was through with them forever.

"But a bunch of years went by, and my dreams were just like everybody else's dreams, I guess. I couldn't see anything special to them; just random stuff from life, no real meaning. And then two years ago, it wasn't long after my wife died, and without any warning, the old dream patterns came again. But this time I started to understand what they were about. When I realized what I was being shown, and I mean when I really knew what I was seeing in those dreams, is when I came to see you."

The sheriff paused and looked down at his hand as he fingered the small piece of stone.

Father Juan leaned his frame forward on the bunk and rested his elbows on his knees.

"Seth, may I ask you a question before you go on with your story?"

"Sure."

"Did you see God?"

Seth Ironwood looked at Father Juan; as he did, he let out a sigh.

"Yeah. How did you know?"

"It just seemed like a natural conclusion. I hear these kinds of stories quite frequently, but most of the time the conclusion is not as clear. Go on, tell me the rest."

"Well after that it really got strange. I really began to question my sanity; you know, where's this taking me? I've always been the type of guy who thought he was in control; especially in control of his mind, but these dreams changed all that. I'd get up in the morning, and when I'd drink my coffee trying to wake up the dream would play itself out again in vivid detail. I tell you, Father, it was like I was still asleep and still dreaming. Sometimes I'd have to stand up just to convince myself that I was awake. Now that's intense, I want to tell you. Then the memory thing started."

"Memory?"

The sheriff paused for a second, and Father Juan knew he was trying to figure out how to say what he wanted to say.

"Yeah. During the day I would see something that would seem like I'd seen it before. I'd have to stop and think about where I'd seen it. Many times I couldn't figure out whether what I was seeing had been in reality or in my dreams. I'm telling you, Father, that's when you really start wondering about your mental state."

"Seth, are the dreams still happening to you?"

"On a regular schedule. I mean I've even got where I think I know that one is coming; I mean when I go to bed, I think I know that night I'll have the dream."

"Tell me about when you saw God. How did you know it was God?"

Seth took a deep breath and again shifted his weight from one foot to the other.

"Father, I was sitting on a chair facing God just the same as I'm facing you now. I mean that. I'm face-to-face with God. It was real. Except I couldn't say anything. I couldn't say a word. I guess you could say I had the opportunity to talk to God, and I failed the test. Can you imagine that? To God, and I couldn't say one blessed word. Not one."

"Maybe, Seth, you simply were overwhelmed to be in His presence. Were you frightened?"

"Father, that's just the thing. I was never scared. You see, He was the gentlest man; I guess you can call Him a man, that I've ever seen. There was nothing frightening about where I was or what was happening to me. Actually, it was just the opposite." Seth fingered the stone owl before he continued.

"The thing about the dream that stood out above all others was His words to me. He said, *You don't have to be afraid*. That's what He said. *You don't have to be afraid*. And, you know I wasn't; I really believed Him."

Seth stopped and chuckled slightly. "That's kind of funny, isn't it? How do you not believe God? But, I still couldn't say a word. In the dream, I always put my face in my hands. I guess I was trying to hide my shame that I couldn't speak. And then, when I would look up; He'd be gone. God was gone."

"Do you remember what God looked like?"

"What He looked like?...that's hard to say. No, I don't really. As hard as I try, I don't see His face. I remember other things though. Strange things. Father, I hope you won't take this in the wrong way, but God was not a very good dresser. I mean, the one detail of how He looked was the loafers. God wore loafers with no socks. And, they looked like they were almost worn out. You know the kind that the leather twists and sags like they've been worn forever; sloshed through the muck, and never polished. Now how crazy is that? God in loafers?

"I don't know where all this craziness comes from. Like I said, for a long time I thought I might be going nuts. But then the dream expanded. Not much, but there was a conclusion added that seemed to give it some meaning;

although I'm still struggling with what that was. And then there was that little bird."

"A bird? What kind of bird?"

Before Seth could answer a shout came down the hall and echoed off the back wall. "Sheriff," the deputy hollered, "The coroner is on the phone; says he's got some important news for you about the Straw case."

Sheriff Ironwood took a deep breath and let it out. He walked to the front of cell seven and shouted back down the hall. "Okay, Bebe. Tell him I'll call him back in a few minutes."

The sheriff turned back to face Father Juan, "It was a wren, I think; just a little wren with his tail pointed up. That little creature somehow made me feel as peaceful as you can feel. But then, he was gone. Just like that, the wren was gone; and with the bird the dream ended. Just like that."

The two men looked at each other in silence for almost a minute. Finally, Father Juan spoke.

"What do you think it means, Seth?"

"I wish I knew. I only wish I knew."

"There weren't any other clues; something in the dream that might help you?"

"The only other thing that makes any sense is the two openings in Heaven; they were like two passages, or maybe doors, I'm not sure. Just before the wren disappears, I always seem to be staring at those openings."

Father Juan raised his eyebrows a little, "Maybe, Seth, that was a choice. I mean God had given you a choice of where to go from there. Could that be?"

"Yeah, I've thought of that. But the trouble is that there is no clue about what that choice might have been...or for that matter, what it is. None."

Father Juan stood up and moved closer to Seth. "You know, Seth, most times when God gives us a choice it is usually a choice about doing the right thing. That's the whole point of the gift of free will. You think?"

"Yeah, Father, I do. You see this?" Seth raised the stone figure and held it between his thumb and forefinger. "Don't ask why, but I just believe that this jade owl that Simon Peter gave me before we went to look for his brother is the key. Somehow I think that if those dreams are pointing, as you say to a choice to do the right thing, and those portals were a way to get there; this little fellow contains that magic. That was a terrible thing that happened to Andrew. I don't think we will ever understand it; not in this life. But as soon as I can find him, I'm going to return this owl to Simon Peter. And I'm going to tell him that I'm sorry we couldn't save his brother."

"Do you think you're responsible for Andrew's death? Is that it, Seth?"

"In some ways, I know I am. It's kind of like the dreams; I can't explain it, but it has haunted me ever since we found him unconscious on that park bench. I just have felt like we should have...I mean I should have gotten to him before it was too late. I should have put more pressure on Simon to lead me to him before he did that overdose bit of theatrics with that Custer reenactor. Doesn't make any sense, does it?"

"Yes and no, Seth. But, you know, there's just a whole lot of things and events in this life that can't really be explained by our reason or logic. And I think this is especially true for people like us who have the job of helping, and in some cases saving people from life's tragedies. We get the job done occasionally, but most of the time we don't. And, no matter how we try to reconcile the facts with our feelings, our rational explanation never really satisfies the soul."

"Do you think God wants us to fail?"

Father Juan shook his head slightly before he answered. "No, I don't. I think He wants us to succeed, but I also think He knows the limits of His creatures, and that He is fully aware that in most cases we won't. But that's just it, Seth; He always is willing to give us another chance. Always. If we make the choice on the side of right, on the side of justice, God will always smile on our effort."

"Well, I hope you're right. One other thing I wanted to tell you. I've submitted my retirement papers. This last event in the life of the sheriff finally helped me to make up my mind to hang it up. This old body has had enough. I'll be putting my badge and gun in the dresser drawer in about a week. The good news is, maybe I'll finally have the time to get through those church courses."

"I'm going to hold you to that, Seth. It might be a better idea than you know."

"Yeah, I think you're right about that too. Well, guess I better go see what the coroner wants to tell me. Thanks, Father, for letting me bend your ear. I've needed to get that stuff off my chest for a long time."

"No thanks needed. It comes with the territory, not to mention the Holy Orders, and I'm glad you did. Let's keep in touch."

The two men retraced their steps along the row of cells to the exit with Father Juan in the lead. As Sheriff Ironwood passed Timothy's cell he thought he heard someone say

Amen. The sheriff stopped abruptly and turned to look at the inmate who stood at the back of his cell.

"Timothy, was that you? Did you just say, Amen?"

The short, bearded man only answered in his usual way with a big toothless grin bordered by thick hair making a comical hole in his beard.

"You old rascal. I'm going to have to have a talk with you someday." The sheriff shook his head slightly as he moved to open the jail's heavy door.

Before the sheriff had closed the door he heard Raaven Stark shout at him from down the hall. As Ironwood turned in her direction, the deputy reached him.

"Seth, we just got a call from the coroner…"

"Yeah, I know I'm going to call him now."

"No, Seth, this just came in. They've got another body up on the Washita."

"Another body?"

"Yes. And, Seth…they think it is Simon Peter."

Sheriff Ironwood stared at Raaven as if she was part of one of his dreams.

"Seth…did you hear me?"

Without a word, the sheriff started down the hall toward the dispatcher's post. He caught up with Father Juan just as he was about to leave the building.

Seth Ironwood put his hand on the father's arm to stop him at the door.

"Father, I'm afraid we need to make another trip to the battleground site. Will you come?"

Father Juan hesitated for just a moment. "Well, sure I will, Seth. What is it?"

"It's Simon Peter, Andrew's brother. They think they've

found the body of Simon Peter Straw," the sheriff all but whispered as he turned back to give instructions to the dispatcher and motioned for Raaven Stark to come with them.

✝

Where the birds go to die

The eighth day of the week

WITH HIS EYES still closed, Seth grudgingly let his right leg slide off the side of the bed and dangle just above the hardwood floor. He felt achy, and he knew he was still tired before he even tried to let his body follow his legs. Lately, ever since he gave up the sheriff's badge and put his Kimber .45 in the desk drawer, he was always tired. Sleep didn't help, nothing did. He knew what it was that disturbed him, but he tried not to let the thoughts come forward, to take hold. They were too vivid, like blood on a white-tile floor.

He stared for a while at the light coming though the slats in the blinds, and at the simple gold cross nailed to the wall next to the window. He felt the urge to offer a prayer, but couldn't think of anything to say so he let the thought fade, and simply made the sign of the cross.

Without looking at the clock he knew what time it was. He always woke up at 7 a.m.; on most days, right as the minute hand pointed exactly between the 1 and the 2. He had been doing this for several months, and at first it was sort of comical. Seth wondered how he could always anticipate the time and look at the clock just as it came to rest on the hour. After a while though the whimsical nature of the occurrence took on a more somber tone, and he dreaded looking at the clock as he came awake. There seemed to be something mocking about the clock face; a mechanical device that was predicting a fate unavoidable in time.

The notion of his morning coffee finally displaced both the tiredness and the dark musings as he reluctantly stretched his frame and walked to the double windows next to the bed. Seth slowly twisted the control rod as the blinds just as slowly revealed the new day outside. The sun reflected off the fresh green of the morning grass; Seth had to squint slightly to control the brilliance that his sleepy eyes were resisting.

He noticed five black ravens working the yard for their breakfast. For some reason, he liked the creatures. They moved with a confidence of purpose; a swagger that impressed the ex-lawman. He watched them for a long moment, and then the old man stretched his back and shuffled mechanically down the hall to the kitchen.

As the one-cup-at-a-time machine began to gurgle, Seth went to the bathroom and relieved himself. He then did what he always did, and washed his face with hot water and a washcloth. As he stared at the strange man in the mirror, a superficial smile, lacking any cheer, greeted his stare. He noticed a small pimple on the end of his nose and squeezed it until it popped; silently he questioned why a man his age still suffered the embarrassment of pimples. Go figure, he thought as he moved back to the kitchen to retrieve the first cup of the sacred caffeine.

As he poured the steamy black three-quarters full and stirred in a mounding teaspoon of raw brown sugar, Seth felt a twinge just behind his left shoulder blade. It was sharp, but mercifully it was fleeting. It wasn't the first time that he had felt it, but the pains were infrequent and only came one-at-a-time so he tried not to pay much attention. To say that Seth didn't like to go to the doctor is like saying the sun sets in the west. He figured the medicos would give him a perfunctory fifteen minutes and an expensive prescription for some pills. Every time he had done that the side effects were always worse than the condition. So now he tried to ignore the pain and filed it away in the category of *hope it goes away.*

Seth turned on the seven-speaker stereo, rotating the volume down to almost nothing before settling slowly into the big leather chair in the corner by the window. He'd taken up the habit of watching the morning traffic going who-knows-where. As he leaned slowly back and brought the mug to his lips, the sharp pain came again. This time it was like a slow drum roll, constant and gaining rhythm and amplitude. Seth jerked abruptly upright, and the scalding liquid ran down the front of his T-shirt. He cussed quietly and jumped to his feet. He stood still waiting for the pain to come again; it didn't oblige and again went into hiding.

"What the hell," he said, and put the cup down on the side table and headed to the bedroom to get dressed. The pain had scared him so he decided to stay busy. He hoped that would be the last of it and grabbed the grocery list off the side of the fridge and made his way to the garage. Seth glanced at his eyes in the rear-view mirror as he backed out of the driveway and came up to speed on the road to town. He noticed his palms were sweaty.

As he came to the steep hill about a mile from his house, the one with the sharp turn just over the crest, Seth noticed a small turtle in the middle of the road. He sped by moving the wheel gently to the right so as to avoid the reptile and watched as the tiny head and beak withdrew from danger. He remembered there was a similar migrant at almost the same spot the week before when he went to town. Then as now he had felt a chilling twinge at the insanity of such a slow moving creature crossing a busy highway. He figured this poor tortoise would most likely suffer the same fate as the one before, recalling the small greasy spot in the roadway as he made the return trip home. Seth drove nearly another mile. The helpless thing stuck in his consciousness like a toothache.

Seth pulled his truck onto the shoulder and stopped. He sat there for a full minute before he turned across his lane and came up to speed in the opposite direction; back toward the little animal, just over the crest of the hill. As he was almost to the spot, Seth pulled over. He looked in the mirror again, but because of the crest he wasn't sure if there was any traffic coming, so he quickly exited the truck and almost ran to the small hard shell that protruded from the asphalt surface like a speed bump. It was resting exactly on the center stripe. Seth aggressively grabbed the creature with both hands and continued on across the road making the assumption that was where the turtle was trying to go. Two cars crested the hill just as Seth, with his bundle, cleared the roadway. He held the turtle at eye level to see if he could get a glance at its head. No luck, it was tucked in tight.

Seth put the hard shell down facing in the right direction and watched its beak slowly emerge from hiding. After all the lack of movement in the road; now clear of the present danger, the turtle moved quickly into the cover of the tall grass. Seth felt again a twitch under his ribs. Strangely the slight pain triggered a thought of how little and helpless everything in this world really is. How threatened.

The lump of olive drab finally disappeared, and Seth was about to turn back when his eye caught a hint of something else obscured by the thick vegetation. He squinted, but all he could see was of a form that appeared to be a dark shadow. Again he was about to turn around when the shadow moved. He fixed his gaze on the spot and took a step just off the shoulder pavement and onto the gentle slope that led down to the bar ditch. As he did, the shadow moved again. To Seth it appeared that it hopped or bobbed or something, he wasn't sure. But now his curiosity was caught, and he took another step closer.

As he did a large tractor-trailer rig rudely went by a few feet behind him, and the air-wash from the massive rig pushed Seth involuntarily a couple of steps down the slope. The shadow moved again; not away this time but toward him. Seth thought maybe it was an animal injured in the grass so he craned his neck to get a better look. He took one more tentative half-step and bent slightly at the waist to peer closer into the grass. As he did, the shadow morphed into reality. It was the biggest raven Seth had ever seen.

The creature boldly, almost with what seemed to be arrogance, waddled a bit closer, clearly absent of fear of the human so near. As it came clear of the grass it, too, craned its feathered neck and intently matched Seth's gaze. Now that he knew what it was Seth hesitated for just a second to study the strangely calm bird not more than a meter from him. It didn't seem to be injured. In fact, the bird was magnificent in its bold blackness. Its dark eyes stared over its abruptly curved beak, and seemed to penetrate into Seth's very soul.

Seth quickly became aware of something else. A presence of some kind; he wasn't sure. He could feel it, and the sensation translated into a slight bodily shake that chilled him. With the chill came a sense of foreboding. Together they frightened him. He uttered a slight sigh, inaudible but still with a bit of desperation in the sound of it. His legs felt weak and shaky.

In reaction, he hastily took two steps backward without being aware that he had moved. He then wheeled and started to climb the slope towards the highway. As he made it to the pavement the shaken man looked over his shoulder and was suddenly startled by the raven as it flew so close to him that the flapping wings brushed his head and the noise of flight strangely registered in his ear. Seth stood frozen in place as the bird began to wing itself in a steep, graceful ascent. First the flight was straight-away across the roadway, but then began a slow sweeping arch into the heavens. As the bird continued to climb into the morning sky, its wings and its trajectory propelled it into the aurora of the early sun. As it did, Seth could see the bird's darkness begin to fade replaced by an absence of color. He couldn't make himself look away even though the sun's intense glare was burning painful circles into his retinas. Unexpectedly the raven became a brilliant white and then it was gone; it had disappeared completely, consumed by the radiance of the distant brilliance.

Seth stood still for a full minute. He was nearly blinded and was reluctant to move until he had recovered at least some of his sight. He repeatedly blinked and rubbed at his eyes trying to stimulate their usual function. As he returned to the pavement, he made an effort to spot his truck parked on the opposite shoulder. He blinked rapidly several more times and then noticed he was crossing the center-line before he even realized he was in the roadway.

Seth first heard it and then as he jerked his head towards the source of the noise; he only had time to make out the big letters across the grill that loomed over him.

W-h-i-t-e.

The message he saw in that small slice of time first was instinctually coded and sent to the brain before it was rearranged into a frightful recognition of its meaning. Seth Ironwood, the tired old sheriff, had no time for a physical reaction; he had no time to be frightened. In that bewildering instant, he only had time to mutter three words, but there was no one to hear them:

"Oh my God."

Then the man who had been Seth Ironwood went home.

Again.

End of Part Two

✝

Epilogue to Part Two

Just ask

✝

Kyrie Eleison

ETH FOLLOWED the crooked path and was surrounded by lush, green foliage that gave forth an aroma that enveloped him in a warm and comforting mist. The faint songs of birds drifted, like the scent, on the air. He strained to listen to the soft noises as he lengthened his stride in anticipation of what might lie ahead. He wasn't sure where he was, but he was aware that he felt at ease.

Suddenly a small bird circled Seth three times and came to rest on his shoulder. It appeared to be a cheerful little creature as it flittered first one way, and then another; using its small, long tail feathers like a rudder. Seth instinctively reached for it, but the bird simply moved gracefully from one shoulder to the other, singing a soft set of notes as it flew.

Seth reached the first turn and took it, and as he did everything that his senses recognized changed, transforming bit-by-bit with each step he took. As he turned to the right, the saturated colors that had enveloped him; the greens, the deep yellows, the brilliant blues, began to fade, first into a pale version of themselves, and then into a transparent glow with little color at all. Finally, all about him was whiteness like no other he had ever witnessed.

He advanced deeper into the strangeness and then felt an overwhelming sense that what would appear next would be a white raven promenading proudly directly in his path. And, although at first, the bird was difficult to see; there it was.

Just beyond the bird, Seth then noticed a small, pine folding chair which appeared to be resting on nothing at all. He approached it slowly. As he reached the hanging chair, Seth stood beside it and waited. He didn't have to wait long for, as if from the fog, a figure was suddenly directly in front of him.

Seth could feel the contours of his face spread, into what he knew must be, a whimsical grin.

"Hello, Seth. Welcome home."

"Hello, Father. It's good to be here." Seth replied quietly.

The small wren once again fluttered from one shoulder to the next before flying away as quietly as a butterfly.

ABOUT THE AUTHOR

RR Carroll lives and writes in the small southwest Missouri town of Neosho. Born and raised in Texas, Ron still retains a slight twang in his speech which is characteristic of native Texans: some traits are not erasable.

Wren is the author's third novel and the second in the *Custer County Trilogy*. The initial story in the series is entitled The Big Lost. The story takes as its theme the controversial re-introduction of the grey wolf into the wilds of Idaho. The third, now in progress, is entitled Cephas. All three tales have as their principle character the sheriffs of Custer County: the first in Idaho, the second in Oklahoma, and the final story playing out in Custer County, South Dakota.

RR Carroll's first novel, Almost Guatemala, is set in the southern Mexican state of Chiapas and portrays a fictional telling of the author's experience while working in Mexico on rainforest preservation in the *Selva Lacandona*. It was this time, during the late 1980s and early 1990s, that inspired him to write.

The author holds a Ph.D. in political science from the University of Nevada, Reno.

OTHER WORKS BY
RR CARROLL

Novels

Almost Guatemala
The Big Lost

available through:
Amazon.com
Createspace.com

Short stories

The Old Cowboy's Box

available through:
Lulu.com

A final note:

If you spend time trying to figure this story out, do me a favor. Take the novel and put it in your lap; preferably in a quiet place while alone. For as long as you can, stare at the eye of the small bird on the cover. Try not to look away, and try not to think of anything else but what you see.

Whatever you see or feel or think; if it is of any significance to you, post it on the *Amazon.com* page where this novel appears.

Thanks and may God's love be with you...

The author.

After all your questions,
After all your doubts,
After all your arguments,
After all your debates,
After all your struggles,
After all your hatreds,
After all your battles,
After all your wars,
After all your destructions.

After all your pain,
After all your suffering;

After all, there remains:

God's love.

Life is a series of stories, good and bad, heroic and tragic, joyous and sad. Here was one of those.

Wren

Wren

Made in the USA
Charleston, SC
21 June 2015